A N

OF
MONS

. . . .

ANGEL
OF
MONS

ROBIN BENNETT

MONSTER BOOKS

Henley-on-Thames . MMXX

Angel of Mons (Monster Books Ltd)

Published in Great Britain by
  Monster Books
  The Old Smithy
  Henley-on-Thames
  Oxon. RG9 2AR

First published 2012; this revised paperback edition published in 2020.

ISBN 9780956868442

A catalogue record of this book is available from the British Library.

Printed by Clays Ltd., Bungay, Suffolk.

This book is dedicated to anyone
who has done their duty –
be they young or old.

• • • •

PROLOGUE

• • • • Dugout

Shells burst overhead, obliterating the darkness in a series of lightening-white flashes that ran all along the battlefront. In the brief silences between the artillery fire someone swore.

Ben watched from the entrance to the dugout as the little corporal with the sad, grey eyes sat down on an empty shell box and blew on his thin hands to warm them. The soldier paused, his face lit in harsh shadows, and then resumed his scratching away at the letter he never quite seemed to finish. At the man's elbow a candle spat and hissed as rainwater found a way through the corrugated roof.

The battle for Mons was only a couple of days old but already the land around the canal was starting to resemble a scene from a nightmare – slopes slick with mud, water-filled craters criss-crossed with hastily dug trenches, all punctuated by the splintered remains of trees.

Ben was afraid but also more determined than he'd ever been in his life. This was his second time in the dugout and he now felt sure he was there for a reason. He also knew that once he left its cramped confines, then the noise of the shelling, the rattling, intermittent fire from the German field positions would be gone in an instant.

It would no longer be 1914 – he would be back in the quiet field over the road from their cheap hotel, and the year would be 2014.

He watched as the dawn slowly came up over the hills in the east, towards the enemy lines – a pink band of light that reminded him of the sunrise on the morning when it had all begun.

• • • •

CHAPTER 1

• • • • Four days earlier

Ben pressed his head against the cool window of the coach, letting the broad fields slip past his fixed gaze as they raced along the dual carriageway towards Belgium. He was already beginning to regret putting his name down for the school trip to Brussels – a typically half-hearted preparation for their Year 11 French GCSEs the following summer.

Things had suddenly gone from looking a bit disreputable to an accident just lurking around the corner when Todd Stelco – otherwise frequently known as, the *Juvenile Defendant who cannot be named for legal reasons* – had decided to come along at the last minute. The combination of him, his new best mate, Banti Croft, and the frankly pathetic crowd control skills of their teacher, made the prospect of a week in Belgium seem to Ben like the start of a road movie where everybody ends up in prison … or worse. Mr. St John would struggle to keep control of a bunch of shy third years from the chess club, let alone two petty gangsters who came from a long line of older and much bigger gangsters all from the same estate in East London.

In Ben's long acquaintance, Todd's hobbies included stealing and making everyone around him do what he wanted. He also went in for violent mood swings.

As for Banti Croft, if the terms of his ASBO had allowed him to go on *Britain's Got Talent*, his star turn would be mugging Simon Cowell for his wallet and shoes, then supergluing the other judges' hands to their faces.

Just to make Ben even more depressed, Steven Fin-shift had puked up on Ben's rucksack on the ferry over and now everything he had with him on the coach smelled of mango-flavoured Fruit Boost sick.

• • • •

Without warning, someone bigger and much heavier than Ben launched themselves into the spare seat next to him, startling Ben out of his daydream, making him bang his head against the window. 'Ben! Beny weny ... Ben ... Benny Bartops, as I live an' breave, how's it ... corr, greezy blud, what's that 'orrible smell?' A slow grin cracked Todd's square face in two. 'Have you crapped in your pants? Tell the troof!'

Ben turned back to face the window, vaguely wondering why the coach had speeded up. 'Crap is what you talk Todd, I smell of puke and it's not mine,' he raised his voice a couple of decibels. '– Finshift should learn to travel on an empty stomach!'

Todd's face assumed a sort of hurt expression (as if anything since the age of about five had ever truly touched him). 'Me talk crap? Aww, don't be like that … anyway, pukin' on your bag, dat's dissing' bruv.' Todd turned around, making a big thing of searching the rows of seats with one of his trademark menacing glares. 'I can sort 'im out ifyoulike.' Todd waited a few moments and when Ben didn't even bother to answer he simply shrugged, putting the matter behind him with a look he probably thought was magnanimous. 'Yeah, well … that's not wot I'm 'ere for.'

Ben turned and stared evenly at Todd for a few seconds who eventually uncomfortable under the much smaller boy's glare. 'What are you planning?' Ben finally asked.

'Well, now,' Todd rolled his shoulders, like a fruit stall trader preparing a pitch on fresh apples with some *luvverly* grapes thrown in. 'Brussels – city of opportunity, mon – rich Froggies, or whatevir, parading demselves about the shops an' stuff. Bit of nickin' … pe'y larceny bruv, so what dewfink? We need someone iccle like you, wiv a bit of experience to get in amongst the crowds, aye … be well trickee to catch, you would. Mon, it'll be *nang!*'

Ben turned back to stare out of the window. His deadpan grey eyes and the discolouration around his temple hinted at a tough background but there was something poised about Ben – an inner calm that had always attracted the type of person who could see beyond the obvious. Like Todd for all his gansta act. Ben sighed almost inaudibly.

'Look, at the risk of repeating myself – I don't do that stuff anymore. And I don't like having to repeat myself, for the record.'

Todd looked genuinely angry – a sort of mottled red patch appeared on his pale cheeks and spread to his forehead and stubbly red hair. For an instant, something flashed in his eyes. If Todd had been in a cartoon, Ben thought to himself, then his pupils would have glowed like coals. Instinctively, Ben shifted position – the showdown he'd been expecting for months looked suddenly imminent. Right here, at the back of the coach. St John would have a major heart attack.

He glanced about. In a confined space like the coach he stood no chance against Todd, so it stood to reason that his only way of avoiding being badly beaten would be to get the coach to stop … Ben made a quick decision – he would break one of the windows with the red safety hammer that was just above his head. He tensed, his thin arms and legs looked scrawny in his school uniform but he was quick and surprisingly strong for his size. Todd tensed too …

... but not this time.

After a moment that could have gone either way for both of them, Todd finally relaxed his features and shook his head. When he spoke again, he dropped the bad Jafaican accent he had been using, on and off, since the start of year ten. 'That's what I don't understand about you B – our dads are doing time together, in the same cell an' all ... you seem pretty righteous one minute, then the next you all stuck up, like yous finking you're better than us on the estate, just cos' your mum's moved off it,' he paused for dramatic effect, making a show of sizing Ben up. 'Blud, are you an' me gonna 'av to 'av words at some point soon ... ?' His East End gangster voice was now on, and he looked like he had something else to say, but Todd didn't get much further.

And nor, as it happened, did the coach.

• • • •

In fact, moments before, Ben had stopped listening to Todd altogether. Something wasn't quite right. Something about the sound of the engine, or the speed or ... he couldn't figure it out right off. But the hairs on the back of his neck rose and sweat beaded his upper lip. Yes, something was well wrong. The coach was coming to a large bridge over a grey river, sign-posted "Deûle".

The way it was heading, it was angled wrong to make it through the narrow gap.

He turned briskly to Todd, who may have basked in a reputation as the hardest lunatic at school, but he had a quick mind that instantly registered Ben was concerned, which meant so should he be. He stopped talking at once.

'We're about to crash into that bridge!' was all Ben had time to shout before there was a sudden deafening explosion caused by a tremendous impact up at the front, followed by the screech and whistle of huge brakes applied too late. The force of the collision sent shock waves down the length of the coach as the air seemed to compress - trying to cram itself into Ben's ears – whilst bags, coats, children and shattered glass flew backwards in a confusing maelstrom all along the seating area.

There was the sound of a lesser impact, which the coach punching a hole through a road barrier just beyond the bridge and now all the children were thrown forwards as the coach rocketed towards the steep embankment. By some miracle, it seemed to avoid sliding into the choppy water that flowed rapidly under the bridge, and carried on down the steep hill. Out of the corner of his eye he saw Banti's nose hit the back of the seat with a loud crack and spray of red, then cold air blasted through the shattered windows and someone shouted. 'It's tippin' over!'

As the vehicle tipped onto its side and slewed into a row of trees, it came to an abrupt stop, the impact brutally punching all the air out of his lungs.

Ben felt something heavy (and very painful) hit him on the temple.

Just before he blacked out, Ben looked out of the broken windscreen ahead and noticed a dark figure, standing quite alone on the edge of the riverbank. Obviously he couldn't be sure, but whoever it was seemed to be looking right at him.

The figure was wearing some sort of cape or poncho that resembled wings as it raised an arm in a kind of salute.

• • • •

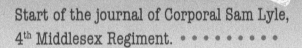
1st August 1914, Calais, France.

Darling Dorothy,

This ain't right. It just ain't. Who am I trying to
fool? I'm a family man now, not a bleedin' soldier
anymore. My place is at home looking after you and the
kids. I took my oath but I did my duty (and much
more, besides) in India then in Africa.

But it looks like this one's a goer and I won't be
called a coward.

So. The Germans have marched across half of
Belgium for reasons I still can't see any sense in and
rumours on the way over had the Frenchies getting the
worst of it in the South. "We'll 'av 'em running back to
Berlin by Christmas Eve, lickin' their wounds!" declared
Parr. Then this officer – tall, Irish Dragoon Guard, all
spit, polish and whiskers – well he over heard Parr
and came over.

"Admire your spirit, Private, but these aren't some
natives with spears or a bunch of stroppy Boer farmers

with hand-me-down shotguns. The German soldier is as well-trained and disciplined as any soldier you're likely to meet – almost on a par with us. You'd do well to remember that when one of them is pointing a bayonet at your kidneys." And then off he went. Poor Parr – he was a bit quiet after that.

Anyway, me and the rest of the British Expeditionary boys got off the Dover troop ship and stood looking out at the channel from the wrong side, if you get my meaning. It was a beautiful sunny day, and Charlie reminded me that it was almost Bank Holiday back home. "Last of the summer's always the best!" he declared, spitting into the dirty grey water in the quay – and I agreed, thinking to meself about how we used to go down to Brighton on the steam train from Waterloo if I had any leave either side. I thought about the last time we were there, back in '12 and the wind blew so strong it felt like it would whip your hair off just like a wig. We still went for a dip though. And I stood on the pebbles with the boys (they were just sprouts then, I remember) shivering, all goose bumps and bones whilst you fussed with the towel, still warm from being sat in the sun on the train.

I had a funny thought ... how come, even on a beach that's all pebbles and rocks, you still get sand in your sarnies?

Mentioned it to Charlie but he just looked at me –

you know the way he sometimes does – like he can see right through you and doesn't much admire the view. Then he spat again and told me that I best stop blathering on and get my kit together, cos' we still had fifteen miles to march before camp.

Just then, some bloke from one of them northern regiments – the Loyal something, I think – comes up to me. "Gis a fag, me ol china," he says, making fun of me cockney accent he must have overheard. Big lad he was, broken nose and you could tell he liked his beer and fighting. I just looks him up and down.

"Jog on," I says but this bloke now squares up to me, standing close, breathing alcohol all over me face. Out of the corner of my eye, I see Charlie slide behind him.

"Last chance, you little cockney runt, before I wring you're scrawny little neck ... god what do they feed you on down there? ... yuv less meat on yer than one of my da's pigeons ... half a mind to chuck you in't that sess pit over there," he grabs me round the throat, "so wat'll it be sparra, stinking shite or a fag for yer northern mate an half a crown for his troobil ..."

Charlie's razor appeared at his throat, glinting in the evening sun and all of a sudden our new friend had difficulty with his words. The razor pressed hard against his Adam's apple for a few moments.

"Now you 'erd my mate," whispers Charlie through his

teeth, "time to move on now, nice an' quiet like and I'll be avin' this an all," he adds, lifting the bloke's wallet out of his trousers. "Ta, ta ... be seeing yer."

Charlie stared coldly at the big geezer's retreating back, pocketed the wallet and shrugged.

"You didn't 'ave to do that Charlie," I said. "I 'ad 'im covered." Charlie wiped his nose.

"Like 'ell you did."

Missing you Dorothy, old girl, and I'm missing the boys and Poppit — I'll do me duty but it's with a heavy heart — you know that. I'm not afraid of being killed, but it's doing the killing that worries me...

It weren't so bad in India, before we had the kids, but then came the Boers and all those dirt-poor families we had to move off their farms and put in cages and after a while every grubby little boy with dust caked in his hair reminded me of little Arthur or our George and every baby that bawled in hunger and fear was little Poppit.

. . . .

13

CHAPTER 3

•••• Inferno

Ben could not have lain unconscious inside the coach for long because, when he woke up, everyone else had started screaming again.

It took him a moment to get his bearings because his brain felt like it was still bouncing around inside his skull, and the coach was now lying on its side. Once he'd got his bloodied, pounding head around the idea that what had been the roof and the floor of the coach were now the walls, it took him a moment longer to realize that this meant the door was blocked. He'd have to find a way out of the broken window without getting cut to pieces.

First thing he did was find a couple of sports tops that had been discarded in the coach. He wrapped one around each hand, making a sort of temporary pair of gloves, and then he started to climb up the seats towards a broken window.

However, try as hard as he could, he wasn't managing hoist himself up and out of the window. It might have been the bang on his head, as Ben seemed to have no strength left in his arms: he felt weak as a chick he'd once seen on the Discovery Channel trying to push aside its shell and stand. But he had to get out. Ben began to feel a knot of fear in his stomach just as he felt a hand with a grip like a power tool grab the back of his sweatshirt and pull him through the window and out.

'Gotcha!' said Todd, actually grinning – like he was finally enjoying the school trip. 'And you owe me one mate.'

The early morning air felt cold on his face as he looked around, vaguely aware of the smell of summer pine, exhaust fumes and something else.

Instinctively, he glanced towards the line of trees but there was no sign of the dark figure. Gingerly, he brushed the shattered glass off his clothes, then he slid down the side of the coach.

As Ben dropped down onto the grass and began to run after Todd, who was heading up the hill towards the motorway, he became aware of two things simultaneously: firstly, the unidentified smell was burning oil and rubber; secondly, no-one else was following them.

Out of the corner of his eye, he saw cars stopping at the top of the slope, about two hundred yards away, where the coach had skidded and gone through the crash barrier. People were getting out of their cars but they were too far to be any immediate use. And nobody on the coach seemed aware that it was on fire. He'd have to go back in to warn them.

Todd stopped and turned as Ben wheeled around. 'Come on, don't be an idiot, we've got to get clear, the petrol tanks gonna catch in a minute and blow your silly 'ed off!' But Ben ignored him.

Ben knew about fire first hand.

His squint, as if staring into the sun and a puckering around his temple signs of a trauma, long-buried in his over-crowded memory.

When he felt shy or embarrassed, he had a habit of holding his hand up against his face to cover the faded burn mark, which usually had the opposite effect of making people stare.

'Electrical fault,' he would mumble, if asked. That, and being locked all day in a flat on his own, aged four.

Ben reached the crumpled side of the coach. For the moment, there was just a lot of choky, sharp smoke rising up from between the wheels as the engine roared with life – the vehicle, lying on its side, looked like some great animal that was unable to get up. The smoke made the back of his throat rasp, but he sensed it was only minutes or perhaps just moments before the smoke became a wall of singeing air, and the bellow of flames as the children inside the coach cried out.

The thought of the flames made him feel sick.

The underside of the vehicle was burning hot, even

through the material wrapped around his hands as he climbed back up, just in time to see Millie Webb look out from the hole in the window Ben had made. 'Mills,' he said in a voice he hoped sounded forceful and in control, 'stick your head back in and tell everyone they've got to get out, NOW – use all the windows. It's not safe to stay inside.' He didn't say why because he didn't want everyone inside to panic and start trampling over one another to get out. Millie – pretty smart – nodded and ducked back inside. By the time Ben had lowered himself back down into the coach, at least five of the class had climbed up on different seats and had started breaking windows with varying degrees of success. Banti had gone one better than everyone, as usual, and had got hold of a fire exting-uisher. Within thirty seconds he had already made a gap big enough for half a dozen kids. People like Banti could be useful sometimes.

Ben grabbed hold of a skinny kid who was climbing past him. 'Zac, see if you can get the driver to wake up and St John, too.' He looked up the coach and saw the driver hanging out of his seat belt, head lolling. There was quite a lot of blood on the window and his face was deathly pale. 'You've got to get as many people to-gether to lift anyone unconscious out!' Then he went over to Banti and asked for the fire extinguisher. For a moment Banti looked like he was going to refuse, but then he saw the determined look in Ben's good eye and handed it over.

Ben didn't hesitate, he climbed back up two chairs and threw the red cylindrical extinguisher out of the window. Then he followed it, just as adults began to arrive from the top of the ridge. A woman in a light brown summer coat tried to grab hold of Ben. *«Non, c'est dangereux, restes-là!»* but Ben just shrugged her off and grabbed the extinguisher that lay in the grass.

Once up at the top end of the coach, he knew just what to do – he'd let loads of these things off in his time at school, usually to create a diversion when Todd was up to something dangerous, or illegal, or both. He flicked off the catch and smashed it against the side of the coach. Instantly a jet of powerful water shot out of the nozzle, which he took a moment to control, then Ben directed it at the pounding engine and the dense heart of the smoke.

He was still going at it, covered from head to foot in black soot, half-dried blood and small burns when the fireman came and gently pulled him away.

• • • •

CHAPTER 4

12th August 1914, Northern France.

Late last night we got to this place near the boarder with Belgium called Amiens. Lieutenant Goddard, who was marching next to me, shook his head, "It's a rum thing, you know – Henry's army marched not far from here in 1415, on their way to meet the French at A Gin Court." (that's what it sounded like anyway). "He was off to fight the French, now we're off to help them out against the Bosch. Same countryside, different enemy. Rum thing."

"So what happened?" piped up Charlie (I knew what his game was – when the officer starts talking you can slow your pace, have a sip or two out of your canteen, perhaps light a fag and generally have a bit of a rest on the move). Lieutenant Goddard seemed lost in his own thoughts for a moment.

"Hmm what?" he says, looking up, "oh, you mean at A Gin Court?"

"That's right, sir, did we lick 'em?"

"Yes, private Gibbs, we actually did, although it looked bad for a bit. Henry wanted more land in France and also that his son be made King of France as well as Britain – the French refused out of hand so Henry assembled a force of about 12,000 – mostly archers and men-at-arms – and attacked Honfleur in August 1415. But he stayed in Honfleur too long and when he tried to get back to Calais he found that the French had rounded up a much larger force, some say as many as 50,000 men, and a lot of them heavily armed knights and nobles who wanted revenge for past defeats they'd suffered at the hands of the English. Anyway, the French effectively blocked Henry's route across the Somme river."

"50,000 against 12,000, sir, sounds like it was going to be a bloodbath, sir?" I pipes up and the Lieutenant nods, a bit patronising-like. (He's just a young chap really, no more than twenty-two or three, I'd say, but I noticed his hair's already thinning when he takes off his officer's cap).

"Hmm, the French thought so too. So much so, they forgot the first two rules of warfare."

"What's that, sir?" Charlie grinned, he's seen more battles than he's had cups of tea but he seemed interested in what the young subaltern had to say. Lieutenant Goddard slowed his pace and starts counting off with his long, delicate fingers that look like they've never been dirty, let alone covered with the dust and dried blood of battle.

"Make sure you've got a better rate of fire and – this is important – a good commander must always choose his ground. The battle lines were drawn by Henry, who may have been young and a bit of a tearaway in his youth but he was tough and by now an experienced campaigner. He needed a way to cancel out the French superiority of numbers, so he positioned his force in a narrow valley between two woods, effectively making a bottleneck.

He also had 7,000 longbow men. Now a longbow – as you may know – was the most feared weapon of its time. Like the modern day Vickers machinegun, it was faster firing and more deadly than anything else around. Each yew bow was over six foot long and it took a strong man with over ten years of training to pull it. Hard work, but a longbow arrow in experienced hands could fire six arrows a minute, faster than any crossbow, travel 150 yards and pierce even the best plated armour of the French noblemen Knights as if going through suet pudding. I remember reading about a knight, William de Braose, who was hit by one, which went through the skirt of his plate armour, his chain mail trousers, his thigh, and then through the leather and wood of his saddle into his horse; when he swerved round, another arrow pinned the poor chap the same way by the other leg!

"Anyway, on the morning of the battle, the French

were too keen and they were dangerously over-confident. The men-at-arms and knights pushed their archers to one side and attempted to rush the English in one suicidal mob across a ploughed field, weighed down with all that brand-new armour and cumbersome equipment. When they eventually got to Henry's infantry, push as hard as they might, they couldn't break the English line that blocked a narrow path through the field and on to victory – they simply got wedged in and shot to pieces by Henry's fearsome archers.

"However, in many respects it was the mud of the Somme that did for the French just as much as the arrows; many knights sank in the quagmire and even drowned in their own armour. Imagine it! – a sea of mud and slaughter – people falling dead and wounded under a hail of fire, the pride and heart of the French army took decades to recover."

"So what happened next, sir?" Soldiers all love a good story and by now all the lads had stopped chatting and, sure enough, some had ciggies in their mouths. Lieutenant Goddard smiled a bit, enjoying his audience, I'd say.

"Well, not long after, Henry V achieved all his military aims, married the French princess Catherine and got thousands of marks in gold for his trouble. Silly thing was, after all that effort and killing, his son – Henry VI – lost it all back in just a few years."

"You know what I think?" says Charlie falling into step beside me.

"What's that?"

"Sounds like the same old story - some top brass King or ruddy Kaiser wants a bit more land, in case they ain't got enough of the stuff already, and he sends the likes of us off to get it for 'im. An' like chumps, we go."

"You fight for King AND country Charlie, remember that." I says.

"Yeah, but it don't change the fact that thousands of ordinary people died on that day at A Gin Court and what - maybe a few hundred big nobs, lords and such like got a bit of a pasting too? It ain't fair, they've always played us for idiots, doing their dirty work for no thanks. But not for much longer," Charlie adds darkly.

Anyway by now it was dusk and we found ourselves coming to a halt sharpish by this dirty great river. Wide n' fast as the Thames, it looked in the gloom. And cold, in spite of the warm weather we'd been having. There must have been about 10,000 of us waiting to cross over by now, with more of the BEF boys arriving by the minute. Then some of the artillery lot turned up with horses and a dirty great cannon.

The Lieutenant, all business now, strode up to this

tall platoon commander ahead and had a chin wag.

"Righty'ho," he says, coming back and addressing himself to me and Sgt Grace, "we're to clear the bridge before nightfall, the Frenchies want us the other side of the Dool river when we camp down for the night," he gave a quick grin in the dark. "Can't say I blame them, we could all do with a bath."

Turns out we got one and all.

I knew something was going wrong when the order came for us to cross and the artillery boys decided to tag along. Horses don't like crossing water at the best of times and there was something about the bridge that spooked them from the start. Anyway, there we were, half asleep on our feet, just thinking about gettin' to the other side, making a brew and getting some kip and suddenly one of our new Middlesex boys, the ones recruited after South Africa – meaning still wet around the ears – well he drops his rifle and off it goes like firework night and shoots one of the horses, hitting him in the flank (your dad would say, "oop tha' arse"). It didn't kill the poor animal but it must have hurt like bloody hell, cos' the oss then decides to bolt, and I don't blame him, except it was our company that happened to be standing about in his way. One minute I'm there on the bridge, wondering if I've got any spare baccy left in me knapsack and the next minute

24

this dirty great horse comes thundering along, hits me full pelt and there's three of us — me, Charlie and Sgt. Grace tipping over the wall and into the inky black waters below.

Now I can swim as well as the next bloke, you know that, but I don't know anyone who can manage it whilst wearing sixty pounds of gear against a fast current. Charlie was lucky and sharp as ever (you're right, stick close to Charlie, he's a survivor and no mistake). Anyway, I saw him start to get the pack off as soon as he went over and chuck his rifle away.

I should have done the same but something caught my eye: a dark figure on the bank. It seemed somehow so out-of-place and it signalled to me ...

Then I hit the water and felt all the wind go out of me. I struggled with me straps but got me fingers all mixed up in the webbing. Just then, I came up to the surface and I tried to get a lungful of air but me pack was too heavy and all I got was a mouthful of water for my trouble before I started to sink again. As I did so, I saw the Sergeant a few feet away but he was sinking fast, his legs thrashing and his hands pulling at his straps. He was going down like back of wet cement. Looks like I'm going that way too, I thought ... oh dear ... dead before the war's even begun ... and I felt this tremendous sadness — I'd never see you and George, Michael and Poppit again ... and, when all's said and done, apart from spending time with you and the kids, what a waste my life's all been ...!

But just as I was blacking out with just my gloomy thoughts for company, I felt a pair of hands grab me from behind and start pullin'.

And not a moment to soon ...

As I got back up to the surface again, I'd already sucked up about a pint of filthy water and I felt weak as a kitten. It's Charlie who pulls me to the shore where people are waiting to help us out.

A few minutes later, as I lay on the cobbled bank, spewing up half the bleedin' river, Charlie puts his face close to mine and grins that grin of his - the one that usually means, I might be your mate but watch out all the same. "Thanks pal," I says, in between coughing n' spluttering in horrible jerky fits.

"No problem, Sam ol' son," he replies, "... wouldn't 'av done that for just anyone though ... you know that, don't you Sam?" Oh, I felt cold all of a sudden - and it weren't just the water.

"Yeah, sure Charlie," I tried to change the subject. "Poor old Sarnt, never stood a chance." I nodded back towards the river. But Charlie just gave me a blank look as if Sgt Grace weren't worth anymore than a stray cat. Then he grinned again and gave me a shove. "You owe me one," he said.

And that shove didn't feel over friendly.

. . . .

CHAPTER 5

•••• Hospital

The details of what happened right after the accident slipped through Ben's mind.

Like the fish he used to catch with his dad and then let go again into the greasy waters of their local canal, he allowed the events to slide off to the dark pools of mind and memory. Ben coped because he had no choice in the matter.

The next thing he remembered clearly was opening his eyes slowly and painfully, lying in a strange bed. At first, he had no idea where he was and then he thought he'd gone blind in the smoke and fire. He thrashed out in a panic and the cover came away from his face, wrapping itself around his forearm as he sat up in the bed, blinking and feeling relieved.

It was night, and orange streetlight reflected fuzzily off a linoleum floor. Ben wrinkled his nose at the unfamiliar smell of antiseptic, polish and about a hundred other, potentially more unpleasant smells that were being kept at bay with cleaning, though they, too, still lurked.

Hospital smell.

Hardly surprising, considering. He yawned and looked about the ward. Sleeping in beds were most of his classmates. They looked different – he'd only ever seen them fully awake, charging about the playground or in uniform, lounging about in class. Ben had never done a sleepover in his life.

His own clothes lay in a neat pile on the chair by his bed as well as his rucksack, which was pretty bloody amazing. It still smelled of puke, though. He scrabbled about a bit and eventually found his mobile phone – there was no signal but it told him that the time was 4.23am. English time, which meant that it was either 3.23am French time or 5.23am – his head still hurt, and they must have given him something to make him sleep and so he couldn't quite remember which way around French time went. Point being, it was morning near enough and Ben didn't want to go back to sleep.

There was a big sticking plaster on his head and both his hands were wrapped in fine gauze and stretchy bandage, expertly taped. His fingers tingled a bit but otherwise he felt pretty OK – all in all.

The possibility of the fire spreading in the coach had scared him more than he'd admit to anyone – and he knew the reason he felt so tired may have been down to what he'd heard described on *Casualty* as concussion or shock. He felt relatively calm now, although perhaps a little homesick, he realised – the thought raising a wry half-smile in the darkness. His old home hadn't felt like home since his dad had been arrested for flogging stolen passports and his mum hadn't even bothered with the new place, which was meant to be a new start but the place was still half empty. It just felt like they'd thrown away everything that was familiar but carefully packed and brought with them all the bad things, including loads of debts and mum's misfiring brain that crushed the life out of her.

He got up and padded, bare-foot, towards the window as quietly as he could. Through the blinds he could see a sort of roof terrace just a few floors below him and the back of the building, which looked like where all the rubbish went; large wheelie bins clustered in groups, like they needed the company – in various states of half full, empty or overflowing.

Beyond the hospital the source of the orange light – a main road – was surprisingly close and Ben could easily make out a signpost about 50 yards away.

Mons.

• • • •

'Well, I must say, of all the places we could have ended up, this is by far the most historically interesting for us, I'm sure you'll all agree!' Mr. St John waved one hand excitedly about (the other had a big blue cast on it and sat in a sling). The walking wounded in the class, those who could be bothered to listen anyway, looked around in doubtful silence: at the half empty car park, the crumbling bypass and the dirty bus stop and wondered if their teacher was still suffering the effects of a knock on the head.

'Yeah,' said Todd, in a stage whisper, 'it's just like Buckingham Palace here.' Todd, as usual, didn't have a scratch on him but pretty much everyone else had some sort of bandage or a plaster or set of crutches. Fortunately, no-one had been seriously hurt and only the driver was still in hospital with a broken leg and a nasty head injury. 'Serves him right,' said Todd who had started a rumour the driver had fallen asleep at the wheel. 'Snoring 'is 'ead off, he was.' Todd told the Doctor when she came to inform them they could leave. As for the driver, whenever he woke he was claiming to have seen a stray horse in the middle of the road, which had made him jump on the brakes and veer.

'Sir?' said Ben, deciding to ignore anything to do with history for the moment. 'Sir!'

'Hmm, yes, what is it Bartops?' Even if it was now common knowledge Ben had reformed, Mr. St John still viewed Ben with deep loathing and squinty-eyed suspicion. Ben couldn't really blame him – since the start of secondary they had made the teacher's life a misery.

'When are we going home, Sir?' Ben had noticed that there was no sign of a coach waiting for them. Everyone turned around to look first at the car park and then the teacher. Something wasn't right.

'Where's our bus?' asked Millie

'Yeah, *Sir,*' said Banti, somehow making it sound like a threat.

Mr. St John's ears went pink. 'Yes, well, ahhm, err …'

'Spit it out, St John,' growled Todd, no longer even trying to be polite.

Mr. St John, who was by now bright red and unpleasantly sweaty, caste about. 'Ah!' he cried, relief suddenly showing all over his face, 'here's Doctor Pouli, she'll explain far better than me.'

'My Gran's goldfish could explain it better than that berk,' said Millie out of the corner of her mouth, 'and it died last Christmas when my uncle fed it some

Quavers.' The joke had been meant for Ben, who was standing right next to her, but their teacher's ears went even pinker.

'Yes, 'ello everybody,' said the Doctor putting her hands in the pockets of her white coat, giving off the distinct impression that the last thing she wanted to be doing was talking English to a rabble of kids in a windy car park. Ben had seen her earlier and knew the type – she smiled with her mouth sometimes but never her eyes. 'Unfortunately I understand zhat our local Poliss *man* want to take a statement from each of you before you go back to your country.' At this there was a brief festival of groans, tribal arm flapping and bag kicking. The doctor carried on regardless. 'Yees, very annoying I am sure but some of you could 'aff been killed and this is a seriously matter.'

'*Seriously* or bloody not, I just want to get back to bloody London. Can't old Bill take a statement when we get back?'

The doctor sighed. 'I 'aff no idea whether zis Beel is authorized to take a statement but I suspect that it will only take a few minutes and the police 'ouse is just over the main road. I am sorry that your little trip was so short, I 'ope you can enjoy what is left of your stay in our town. It is not the first time it 'as been taken over by a gang of unruly Briteesh. If any of you need any more medical assistance you know where I am.' At this she put her head down and marched off.

'Wot does she mean by *our stay*, Sir?' asked Banti, almost astonishingly first on the ball.

'Yes, well, I'm afraid that as you can see class, the matter is entirely out of my hands.' St John sounded whiny and more than a little relieved that he could almost legitimately put the blame on someone else. 'But I also have more bad news –'

'So you won't be dying of your injuries after all, Sir?'

'Yes, ha, *ha*, very droll Mr. Stelco … no I'm afraid that the coach company is being a little bit difficult. There is a replacement coming from Bordeaux today but unfortunately it is nearly full. This means that after you have made your statement, not all of you will be able to fit into the existing free places.' There were more snorts of disgust and groaning at this, so that Mr. St John had to raise his reedy voice a few octaves. 'All those with injuries which need further medical attention will be of course first to go! This leaves Croft, Stelco, Bartops, Millie Webb, Zac Gamble, Lucy Pint and me, of course!'

'So how long are we going to be here?' asked Ben.

St John looked as if he heartily wished Ben's mouth and not his hands were bandaged up but he answered because, as Ben had come to realize a long time ago, that's what teachers were basically paid to do – answer kids' questions, however stupid, or annoying. 'Um, yes ... the travel company is sending another coach to pick us up in three days. BUT,' he raised a long white finger to forestall anymore loud complaints, 'I have taken the liberty of booking us into a very comfortable Bed & Breakfast, all at the coach company's expense, and I can assure you that the next few days together will be fascinating and very educational. This town was part of the German assault during the First World War. The scene of the very first battle between the British Expeditionary Force and the German advance.'

'I take it you mean the Schlieflen Plan, Sir?' asked Todd.

Everyone looked surprised, not least Mr. St John. However, Ben might have known that Todd would be a keen student of warfare. 'Yes, yes, quite so Mr. Stelco, I can already see that you'll be taking this opportunity to brush up on your history.'

'That's not all I'll be taking the opportunity to do, bruv,' remarked Todd, looking pointedly at Ben.

• • • •

'What a nerve, I can't believe that St John didn't even thank you,' said Millie, falling into step with Ben as he crossed the road.

'Thank me for what?' Ben was genuinely mystified.

'Come on Benedict Bartops – *Mr. Reluctant Hero* – if

it wasn't for you, the bus could have gone up in flames, with all of us in it. We'd be cheese on toast. This could have been a tragedy, not just a pain in the whotsit.'

'I didn't do much,' he said. In fact Ben couldn't shake the feeling he'd over-reacted to the fire, which was never that bad. He'd been the only one even slightly hurt by it, all the other injuries on the coach were from the crash itself. He cringed inwardly when he saw himself frantically hosing down the non-existent flames, then having to be carried away by the French fireman who probably had a good laugh about the hysterical English kid and his miniature extinguisher. Ben's hand hovered by the side of his face. He saw Millie looking at his old burn mark and so he deliberately turned his head away.

'It's OK, you know,' she said as they walked up the gravel path to the B&B. 'You can hardly see it ... and I think it looks cool.'

Ben really didn't know what to say to this so he shrugged. And then he scowled when Millie smiled at him.

• • • •

He made his statement to a *Gendarme* via an interpreter – a nice Dutch lady with perfect English – who left her children in reception whilst she worked. Then

Ben was on the phone to his mother.

The local police had lent them a private room with a bare desk and an old-fashioned phone to make the calls back home. Most of his class had kept their conversations to a minimum, each getting off the phone in under five minutes. For Ben, there was no chance of this. Calls to his mother could be anything between thirty seconds and three hours.

It was the middle of the afternoon when he phoned and she sounded bleary, and only half-listening. This was usually a bad sign and at first he found it hard to get through to her what had happened. 'Mum, the accident was here. In France ... I mean Belgium. Nothing's wrong with the flat, how would I know?'

The penny dropped. 'Oh,' was all she said, a small exhalation, like a frightened animal. 'You're hurt.' She sounded bereft. It was as if someone else was telling her Ben was dead or something.

'No Mum, I'm fine.' Ben lied.

'Your little friends, their poor parents ... '

Ben pressed the cool, plastic receiver against his head for a moment and stifled a sigh. 'No it's alright, they're fine as well – a few cuts and bruises. Todd's fine – can you tell his mum, I think he's used his call to phone his dad.'

There was a long pause, then a sharp inhalation of breath and an abrupt change in tone. Ben sensed a mood-swing … this could go either way, he thought. 'OK! My love – then you must be strong for me!'

Super Mum was now on the line.

Ben honestly didn't know what was worse.

'Sure, Mum – we're all OK – really we are. We'll be here a couple more days whilst they arrange a coach for us. Mr. St John, you remember him – orange wife, she works in the new salon in the high street – he's got loads of history trips planned for us around Mons.'

The rest of the conversation was OK, his Mum just remembering to ask Mum things, like whether he had enough clothes and if he had somewhere to stay.

However, he did briefly wonder about the last thing she said before she rang off, which had sounded completely mad but at the same time, it was pretty unlike her to drift back like that so quickly. 'Mons? … oh, yes, I remember – the angel – *The Angel of Mons*. I saw something on TV about it a long time ago.' Her voice had gone dreamy again. 'He must have protected you.'

• • • •

CHAPTER 7

Extract from the journal of Corporal Sam Lyle, 4th Middlesex Regiment. • • • • • •

18-21 Aug, Northern France and into Belgium

So there I am, lying on this cold slab of concrete, still coughing me poor throat out, wishing I had drowned, when this little scrap of a private in a Middlesex tunic three sizes too big comes up.

"Are you alright, mister?" he inquires.

I looks 'im up an down. "Shouldn't you be at home with your mum?"

"I'm eighteen," he replies, bit defensive.

"Sure," I says, "and I'm the Sugar Plum Fairy an' all."

He just shrugged and starts pulling me sleeve – gentle like but firm (there was more strength in him than you'd have thought). "Best get you by a fire to warm up, you'll catch yer def lyin' 'ere."

I tried to get up on me own but then I sort of staggered a bit sideways, so this young feller has to catch hold of me, stop me falling back in the water.

"Cheers," I said, having a look about, wondering

39

where Charlie had got to, and I meant it – there was something about the kid. "What's yer name son?"

"Private Heater... er... sir!" he replies, suddenly remembering my rank.

"Well, private, have you got some baccy in that pouch of yours, or just sweets?"

So the next morning, right after me first brew and ciggie, I'm off to see the Quartermaster for some new kit. It's barely dawn and everything's sort of grey in this light and my uniform's clammy and 'orrible, but the Quartermaster's been up for hours and he's got the temper to prove it. Fat geezer (they usually are), he huffed and puffed a bit but eventually I got what I needed.

Well! You should see me now, Dorothy my dear, you'd be that proud – I look like a bleedin' cavalry officer. I've got a lovely new set of webbing to hang me cartridge belt with 75 rounds of your 303 ammunition, shiny new bayonet, mess tin (though I'll miss the one I lost the night before). I needed a new greatcoat, a blanket – 'cept the one the QM gave me's second hand and smells like a cat's been using it. And of course me iron rations: Tin of Bully beef, oxo cubes for soup, biscuits, some salt, sugar and half an ounce of tea – and I'm not allowed to touch any of it unless an officer says I can!

Best of all, got me new rifle. I know you're not interested in all that, except when I tell you it's the one thing, apart from Charlie, most likely to keep me alive out here. I can still fire nearly thirty rounds a minute and I can knock the apple out of a chap's hand at 200 yards, even if that does sound like boasting. Firepower! The Lieutenant was right, after India and the Boers, all of us experienced soldiers out here know that's what counts.

"Take good care of that one," the Quartermaster growls, his double-chin wobbling, 'an don't decide to go swimming with it on again – it cost 'is Royal Highness near enough three quid."

Had mixed feelings when I shrugged my new pack on – it's like lugging a dead sheep about on me back – almost half the weight of a grown man it is.

I met my new mate, young Pvt Heater, coming out of a communication tent (looks like our platoon commander has seen some sense and made him a runner – that way the young lad'll be safe from any of the heavy fighting, if we see any – that is). He nearly knocks me over. "Watch where you're going, or I'll put you on a charge!" I bark.

"Sorry, Sir! Pooh, that blanket doesn't half pong." (Cheeky begger).

"Where are you going in such a hurry?" I ask.

"Shouldn't really say," he looks a bit sheepish but proud of hisself at the same time, peering about like he's in the music hall, "but I've got some bad news – orders to take it to the Sir John French 'imself ... if he's up."

"Of course he'll be up – he's got 70,000 men to look after and so you better be on your way to him sharpish." I replied.

Heater stiffens to attention. "Course, Sir, yes Sir, begging your pardon!" He makes to dash off but just before he does he leans over and whispers (he's got these brown eyes, all earnest, just like that Spaniel the blacksmith kept). "Brussels has fallen," he looks around again before continuing, "there are reports of more civilians being shot by the Bosch. Terrible things ... just like in Liege ... killing ordinary folk ... an' more kids, I shouldn't wonder."

And with that he darts off, all elbows and knees, jinking through the soldiers who are sitting about, smoking over their billy cans, weaving around the tent poles and equipment. He's long gone before I can take it in and ask him anymore.

I don't know, Dot, the bad feeling about this one has just got ten times worse. Many of the boys only signed up because of what they heard the Germans had done to those poor nuns and before we left I heard they had burned Liege to the ground with civilians in it. It seems like war isn't just for the soldiers anymore - Gawd knows I saw that in South Africa - old men, women, children all get caught up in this business now. Somebody said that if the Bosch make it to Boulogne then they can send these new dirty great cannon shells of theirs all the way to London. If that happens, you've got to promise me you and the kids'll get out to your dad's in Halifax.

Africa, India and now France - where will it end?

I made a promise to myself - I'll get back to you somehow. Whatever happens out here.

And a promise is a promise.

Well, once we got underway, marching south from Amiens, I felt my spirits lift as the sun came up. and I didn't breath a word about what they say had happened in Brussels to the rest of the lads, I didn't want to get the young lad in trouble.

Eighteen miles a day almost felt easy with the sun on your face and a cool breeze. Lunchtime we stopped at a village and some of the locals came out with these huge great flagons of red wine the frenchies all drink from in the flicks. The drink went straight to me head, I was that thirsty.

We got ourselves a new Sergeant (Trisk is his name, looks like the last action he saw was the Crimea but you still wouldn't want to bump into him down a dark alley). He tells us that we're not likely to be involved in any fighting.

"We're just here to support the Frogs - The Times woz saying they've got over a million soldiers meeting the Germans, so there prob'ly won't be much fighting for us to go around, I expect." (At this some of the new lads kicked their heels a bit and grumbled - as if getting shot at was something to look forward to - "What are we come all the way 'ere for then Sergeant?" "How long to we have to 'ang about 'ere then, if we've got nothing to do?" "Might aswell 'av stayed put in Blighty.")

The new Sarge (got this great big waxed moustache, looks like he brought it in a joke shop on the pier) glares at a couple of them and the lads catch on quick and simmer down. "You're 'ere because that's where yer being told to be and as long as yer still breeving and you can accept the Kings shilling in yer grubby ungrateful paws, then that's where yer staying. Most likely the Frenchies will stop them in their tracks and our job will be to help finish them off with a bloody big cavalry charge all the way to Kaiser Bill's front room. There's only 70,000 of us out here but we're still the best professional army in the world ..." he jabbed his great big finger at us. "Not that you'd guess it, looking at the present company!"

Anyway a couple of days later we're marching through a place about forty miles south of Amiens. By now, rumours and news of Brussels has reached most folk in the countryside around here and there's panic in all the towns and little inhabited places (I won't say "village", most are just collections of these little bitty houses thrown up around some ploughed fields, so not really anything).

I get a sense of something I don't know how to describe ... something about to happen.

Something terrible.

Most of the lads don't seem to notice it but I feel it, same as I feel the wind on my face. I know what you're thinking, but even you've learned to trust my little "hunches" as much as I have over the years – remember that time I got into a panic for no reason and picked Poppit out of her perambulator? Just as well too, that cab would have crushed her.

Anyway it's not just a hunch – the boys might seem to think it'll be over before Christmas but the frenchies don't, leastways not the civvies and they're scarpering by the truckload.

Half of them start by trying too leave with everything – even kitchen cupboards and chicken coups. Then they get a few miles and they realize that it's hopeless, so they start dropping things – beds, chairs, grandfather clocks, lamps – all by the side of the road. One time we had our own parlour when we stopped – kitchen table, comfy chair each, couple of rugs and an empty parrot cage on a big brass stand. All indoor stuff but outside! Charlie and I even found a small picnic basket with mewling kittens curled up on a dirty pillow, can't have been more than a few days old. Regulations don't let us take anything (most of the stuff is just junk anyway or too large to carry) but it felt wrong leaving those kittens behind.

We come to this village (by now our BEF brigades are spread out over about twenty miles of road, and us lot in the Middlesex are in the vanguard, shadowing the scouting parties) and there's not a soul there, just an empty street, a thin dog nosing around the side of a house and this donkey braying its silly head off. It shuts up when it sees us and by now we've all gone a bit quiet, too ... it's early evening and the sun is beginning to sink behind some barns where a wind has just got up. There's a sort of low moaning noise coming through its missing roof tiles and the open shutters. One of them suddenly bangs open and Charlie, whose been marching next too me all day, nearly jumps out of his bleedin' skin. Makes me jump an all.

"I don't like it 'ere," he remarks and I've more than half a mind to agree.

So there's me, Charlie and the Lieutenant at the front, looking down an empty street; then the dog looks up and barks. Just once.

So I peer up the street and from nowhere there's a figure standing in the middle of it, right where there was not a living soul before.

We carry on marching and as we get closer, I see that it's just an old lady, dressed head to foot in black, a thick woollen shawl around her head, in spite of the heat, like a monk's thingy. She shows no sign of shifting, so the Lieutenant signals us to stop.

No-one moves nor says anything, we just stand there listening to the wind, feeling a sort of pressure build and she stares at us with these dull rheumy eyes of hers. Then she hawks and spits and starts to talk in broken English. Her voice is quiet at first but it carries through the ranks better than any sarnt-major on a parade ground. Perhaps it was the wind.

"... Ze Prussians, zey came when I was just a little girl.

"And they took my papa out and they shot eeem. Then zey took our owse because it was zeeh beegest in ze village and zey made my mama cook and when she refuse zey beat her but steel she refuse, so zey beat me and only then she cook and clean ... and she cry ... we all weep ... for my dead papa and for what 'as become of us. Then the Prussian zey left but my seester said zey would come back and she cry at night and then she ran away when she was just ten year old and we never see 'er again." She stopped here, and I thought she was done but she was only drawing a big breath ... for what comes next.

When she next opens her mouth it's a horrible screech and all I can see is her black teeth and gums like an old sheep as she retches out the next bit, like the words were making her sick.

"And now I look at you Breetish," then she points her finger with its chipped nails right at Charlie, "with your big boots and peenk faces and I see that you are just like zem. Soldiers! you are all the same, murderers! Killing zhose zhat are weaker zhan you.

"But you are zher DEAD! I see you marching through 'ere, when evereebodee 'as left me and all I see are your putrid corpses! Beeg stupeed corpses walking down the road ... rotted skin 'anging off your faces, bullet 'oles, like craters in your stomach, filled with worms. Your eyes are like feesh eyes, your tongues grey, and fat with rotted puss...!"

"Come on! I think I've heard enough." said Lieutenant Goddard, breaking the spell and we start to file around and past her, scurrying away like we was back to being small boys, like we was running away from our worst nightmares.

As I left the village, I turned to look at her again - standing there, shaking with fury.

"YOU ARE ZHE DEAD!"

When I look at Charlie, I see he's sweating and it's not just the heat and he's shaking too. I ain't never seen him like that — nor's anyone, I'd say. Somethings changed in him since Africa and he worries me.

That night we marched until we got to a middle-sized town, sat on a hill.

"Mons" said an old sign.

And it was funny, just as we passed it the light seemed to change, like everything was lit up orange. The road surface suddenly looked black and kind of shiny and just for a second a new sign seemed to hover behind the old. It still said "Mons".

The next morning we wake up in the main square, my back aching something rotten from sleeping on cold cobbles all night. There's a big old church looming over us with an odd tower. "The top on that thing looks like the urn they put my Auntie Edna's ashes in," Charlie remarks. George has got a brew going when the Lieutenant comes up.

"I'm to take our company out on patrol this morning, so once you've finished your tea we'll have to be off. We'll be shadowing some of the chaps from the Royal Irish Dragoons." Charlie lights his fag, making the new Sergeant scowl from a few feet away (even after India it's not seen as respectful to smoke in front of an officer, even in the field).

"That mean we'll say how dee doo to any Germans, Sir?" he asks. Always a nose for trouble, our Charlie. But the Lieutenant shakes his head.

"Very unlikely, Private Riley - they were last spotted over 60 miles from here. We're trying to rendez-vous with the French, find out what we can do to help."

"Ron Day who?" That was George.

"Means meet up, fat head," growls Charlie.

Half an hour later we're going up the hill to a place called Casteau. We're having to do it at the double, cos the Dragoons are prancing about on their big shiny horses and Sergeant Trisk wants us to keep up. Even with us running like idiots, we're a good three hundred yards behind them when I hear a shot ring out from one of our boys ahead.

We all stop dead in our tracks, peering through the sparse trees that sprouted all higgledy piggledy at the end of the road. Then we see a few of the Dragoons break away and charge on horseback towards a group of soldiers who have suddenly appeared on the crest of the slope. Looks like they're on bicycles. "I bloody knew it!" said Charlie. "I just bloody knew them trees would be teeming with Bosch. Sixty miles?! More like six!"

In the morning sunlight we caught glimpses of grey tunics and oddly-shaped headgear. Our first sight of the Bosch! And I suddenly felt a bit funny ... I'd only just realized something ... these German scouts running away from our cavalry on push bikes are just like us — they live in the same sort of houses, eat the same food (more or less), go to the same church ... half our royal families even bleedin' German, if you listen to Charlie. Young Heater (we've taken him along just in case we need to get a message back to the command centre in Mons) has gone a bit pale but looks more excited than the rest of us put together. "My dad says we'll be the first British troops to fire a shot in anger in France since Waterloo. Except then the Germans were on our side and we was fighting the French. It's a funny old world cometofinkofit. My great, great granddad, he fought in Waterloo ... Infantry man too ... same as my granddad and his son, my dad ... we've still got his medals from France, bit tarnished and the ribbons gone manky."

"Thankyou, Heater, that's enough." Sarge rested a knarly old hand on the lad's shoulder.

No-one heard the shot when it came. Not until Private Parr fell down anyway — even then it sounded like a crack, a harmless noise like a stick breaking under your boot.

But poor Parr was standing right next to me when the top of his head seemed to lift off.

"Oh," he said, almost like he was puzzled, like he'd

just lost his keys or forgotten where he left his bike.
And then he died. Just like that.

Heater was sick and then all hell broke loose up
ahead.

"Looks like they've caught up with them!" said the
Lieutenant with some satisfaction. There seemed to be
very little actual fighting going on, just a lot of shouting
and men sticking swords under the noses of other men
who had their hands in the air. Charlie had hit the
deck, guessing (rightly in my view) that whoever had
shot Parr wasn't part of the same bunch who was
surrendering to our boys up ahead.

However, the Sergeant leans over and grabs Charlie
by the scruff of the neck, hauling him up. "OK Private,
look sharp and get that body wrapped in his ground
sheet!" The Lieutenant (looking a bit peaky himself,
although there really weren't that much blood, to tell
the truth) seems to come out of himself.

"Quite right, Sergeant! We've lost poor Parr but our
boys have got themselves some prisoners by the looks of
things. We've come off best in this engagement,
I don't think they were expecting to find us here
either, so surprise is on our side. Heater?"

"Yes, Sir!"

"Wipe your face, then why don't you dash down the
hill and let the CO know what's just happened. They'll
have heard the shots and no doubt they'll be wondering

what's up. Tell them we've taken one fatality but otherwise it looks as if we can get our men into position before the Germans have a chance to work out we're all here."

Charlie ain't so sure though. "If them's the divisions that's come from the South, then there could be as many as 150,000 of them over the hill and there's barely 40,000 of us arrived. I don't much fancy those odds. It'll be a massacre ... mark my words."

Anyway, we didn't get much time to reflect on that before the Lieutenant orders us to get out of Casteau sharpish and into position down the hill by the canal.

So it's started.

Charlie's right. God help us all.

• • • •

CHAPTER 8

· · · · Todd

The fire hissed and spat in the corner, like a bad-tempered tomcat. Bad enough if it was a log fire, but this one was electric.

Students and teacher looked at it for a bit in perfect silence and then turned to study the hotel proprietor who was slouched, face down, on the counter. At first it occurred to Ben that the man may *actually* be dead and they were the first to discover him – judging by the smell, he'd been there some time. Then the corpse uttered a loud snore and a thin stream of saliva dribbled from the corner of his mouth, making a small pool on the grubby Formica.

'I'm not stayin' 'ere Sir, it's an elf 'asard.'

'*H*ealth, Stelco, it's pronounced, *health* with an aitch, same as *hazard*. And I'm afraid we are staying here – *elves* notwithstanding – because this is all we can afford. If anyone's parents can stump up the cash for the Holiday Inn over the road – by legal means or not.' He shot a snide, semi-triumphant glance at Ben, ' – then I'll be first over the road with my toothbrush and teddy.'

At this point, the sleeping man at the counter suddenly sat bolt upright, blinked (rapidly) twice and broke into a huge toothy grin. 'Bienvenue, les Britishes!' he exclaimed brightly, for all the world as if he'd merely been resting his eyes. He spread his arms wide, leaving everybody in no doubt as to where the awful smell was coming from. 'Welcome to ze Hotel Belair, ma 'umble habode.'

'Well, Stelco' said Mr St John, marching briskly up to the counter and signing the register before anyone else could offer any more objections, 'he can't pronounce his aitches either – you two should get along famously.'

• • • •

Ben spent the rest of the day mooching around what little there was of the town, avoiding Todd who'd been making *I want a word with you* faces ever since they had left the hospital.

Unfortunately, at around 7pm, his luck ran out.

Bored, Ben had wandered away from the main part of the town and he was now going down a narrow cobbled road towards what looked like a broad canal with steep concrete sides. He'd seen Millie from a distance, sitting in a café with Lucy Pint and Zac Gamble. They looked like they were stuffing their faces with pancakes. Ben, who had barely ten euros on him to last the next couple days, waved noncommittally and kept going. He'd managed to work out from the French instructions in their room that breakfast was included at their hotel and he'd buy some crisps later to stave off hunger.

His mum *had* promised him more spending money but, when it came time to leave, she didn't mention it and Ben hadn't the heart to insist. He'd worked it out and he could eat OK on a couple of euros a day – if he really went for it at breakfast.

• • • •

He'd been sitting by the canal on a metal bench for about half an hour, watching the sun go down, when he heard a soft tread on the gravel behind him. Ben didn't bother turning around. 'Hello, Todd,' he said, 'lost your Rottweiler?'

'I take it you mean Banti?' said Todd, sitting down. Good sign, he was talking normally. He offered Ben a choice from a handful of sweats he'd pulled out of his jacket pocket. There was no bag, so Ben assumed they'd been stolen. He hesitated for a moment, then took one.

'Thanks … yeah, that's him.'

'He's back at the hotel, still on painkillers for his noggin'… they make 'im sleepy. Bless. Anyway,' Todd looked aggressively at Ben who forced himself to relax, whilst keeping an eye out for a possible escape route, 'what you got against him? Least he knows who his mates are.'

'He's an idiot,' Ben's voice was flat. Todd paused for a moment to consider this opinion whilst sucking noisily on his sweet.

'Yeah, you're right,' he said, grinning, ''e is a bit fick as it 'appens.' Ben picked a stone up and threw it in the canal, as his other hand moved towards Todd's coat pocket, cool and fast. 'Don't know why you should 'old that against the bloke, though, 'alf of our school can't write decent English.' Ben popped a cola fizz in his mouth and shrugged. It took a moment for Todd to realize what had just happened. 'You crafty little sod … you just picked my pocket!' He ruffled Ben's hair and for a moment it was almost like being back to best mates again; aged seven, sitting by another canal – in London – fishing for old boots, shopping trolleys and dead cats. Later they'd nick all they could eat from the local cash and carry and then they'd go home and tell their dads about it. Who'd be really proud.

But, in a moment, the moment passed.

With little or no warning, Todd thumped Ben's arm, harder than could strictly be considered playful. 'So, Bartops, 'bout what we was cooking up on the bus before we was so rudely interrupted by imaginary 'orses …'

'The answer's still no, TS,' replied Ben before Todd could go any further. He had a sort of vague hope that using Todd's old nickname would soften his former friend up. It didn't. A sudden red flush of anger showed briefly on his pale cheeks and he made a show of smoothing down his closely-cropped red hair, as if thinking. But it was an act, a feint. With a turn of speed that would do credit to a pro boxer, Todd's other hand shot out and slapped Ben in the face before he could react. He looked coolly at Ben. Pure *gangsta* again.

'That slap was just playful like … you know that don't you Ben?' Todd licked his lips. 'So, let's start again shall we, eh?' Ben, who had pushed himself back to the limit of the bench, so that the metal frame now dug painfully into his kidneys. He felt half-caged. He glanced around: there was hardly anyone about. He should have stayed in town. Ben also knew, from past experience, that Todd reacted to fear in others like a predator – no mercy, just aggression, so he nodded but he kept his eyes on Todd's face and not his hands. Todd took the nod to be a good sign. 'OK, so you're back on board then … good decision …'av you seen how many tourists there are here – cameras, great big day bags they leave lyin' around their feet when they stop to 'av a drink or look at a map … they must be slow or somfin'.'

Ben swallowed – his mouth felt as if it was clogged

up with dry sand. He had the nasty feeling he was about to sign his own death warrant but it couldn't be helped, he'd promised his mum and he couldn't risk letting her down, not now, not after everything else. 'I don't nick stuff anymore, Stelco. I already told you.'

This time Ben was ready for the punch and when it came he ducked slightly one way and then bobbed to the right as Todd's other fist hooked around. The second punch almost found its mark, just clipping Ben's forehead but he hardly felt it. One of Todd's dad's dozen or so less-than-savoury occupations had been a bare-knuckle boxer and he had taught both of them in their flat in Leyton. And Todd was a natural with his fists, meaning that Ben knew that if Todd got to his feet first, then he'd might as well curl up and hope the beating was a quick one. All that lay between the two of them was a half-drunk bottle of coke on the bench. But, if Todd was anything, it was vain (as well as violent and unreasonable). In desperation, Ben grabbed the plastic bottle with both hands, and got the desired effect.

Coke erupted over Todd's leather jacket, t-shirt and face, buying him some precious time.

A second or perhaps less was all Ben needed and he was up and out of the seat like a rabbit. Ducking a badly aimed fist, he shot off, kicking Todd in the knee as he went – very hard – just for good measure. Todd roared and looked almost comically incredulous that anyone would dare cover him with coke and then kick him all in the space of a few moments. In any other circumstance Ben would have agreed but desperate times called for suicidal measures.

By now, it was dark and he ran along the canal, heading for an area in the middle distance where the streetlights petered out. He had about twenty yards on Todd, who had now stopped hopping around on the spot, swearing and was picking up speed as he charged after Ben.

If he could just get to the darkness on the edge of town, he might be able to lose Todd.

Ben was usually faster than Todd, but he knew he was going to tire out very soon. He still wasn't feeling that clever after the crash – added to which he hadn't eaten all day. At first he seemed to be pulling away from his ex friend, but gradually the sound of Todd's feet got louder. 'You're deader than dead Bartops!' Ben made an attempt to speed up but the extra effort just made him weak and light-headed. So he forced himself to slow down, if he could get into a rhythm, he might be able to out-distance Todd. The pools of darkness under the trees still seemed incredibly far off and Ben briefly considered running towards town – amongst people – but he'd seen enough muggings to know that civvies hardly ever got involved in violence until after the event. 'I'm gonna pound your face until it looks like a half-eaten burger, even your mad mum won't recognize you!'

Suddenly he was up almost level with Ben who felt a hand grab at his collar, slip and then snatch at it again. He arched his back and Todd's fingers closed on thin air, just millimetres away as Ben felt the wind they made on the back of his neck and got a brief spasm of goose bumps. Two more paces and Todd would have him – and he had really no idea now if he was feeling weak with fear or exhaustion. Feeling sick and on the verge of collapse – his vision tunnelling – Ben used the last of his energy to jink right and launch himself into the canal.

As he hit the water, he blacked out.

• • • •

CHAPTER 9

• • • • Pre Birth

When he opened his eyes, Ben was still below the surface. No sooner had he realized this than his mind started to drift back to unconsciousness. He almost felt relaxed: hanging there, suspended in water – like a spaceman in stasis. His mind seemed to float, too, and he felt something that he might have described as *reality* slip … away from him and fall into the murky depths, un-mourned. Reality had never done Ben any favours.

Something else, something different, drifted in on the current and replaced it with a different consciousness. There was a shift of time and place.

Ben opened his eyes again. Grey murk clouded his vision but he could have sworn that now there was someone else under the water beside him. For one awful moment, he thought it was Todd but, as he thrashed out in panic, the vision faded and his hand caught hold of something. Something real. Despite the dirty water stinging his eyes, he peered at what looked like an old-fashioned army belt and he kicked upwards.

A flash of orange that Ben at first took to be a

flickering street light burst above him. Three more kicks and Ben broke surface just as an explosion tipped his world on its axis. It sounded like nothing he had ever experienced first hand before – like the whole world was suddenly a car bomb except it had just gone off in his own head and it the sound waves battered the surface of the water. The explosion was so loud, he seemed to lose his vision and all co-ordination for a few moments. Ben grabbed for the concrete of the bank, finding only mud, as what sounded like a burst of heavy machine gun fire clattered above the ringing in his ears and made him duck back below the water.

Something was very, *very* off here. He associated these sort of noises with television and computer games, not his own life. What had just happened since hitting the water? It sounded like war had broken out. Ben looked this way and that, half expecting to see Todd on the other bank but he saw nothing, just dark lines of unfamiliar trees occasionally lit by flashes.

He went to pull himself out of the water as another explosion splintered the night in blistering light and deafening noise. Ben, who was getting colder by the second, grabbed at the bank and hoisted himself onto the wet grass, hope rapidly fading that this sudden nightmare would dissolve as some easy explanation made it all go away.

Another shell burst nearby and he forced himself to

his feet, running at a crouch he'd seen soldiers use on the news, towards the top of the embankment. *'What's going on? What's going on? What's going on? What's going on? What's going on? What's going on? What's going on? What's going on?* he repeated like a mantra as he scrabbled up the slope, reaching the top in seconds. He flinched as individual rifle fire zipped only a few feet above his head. Then came another explosion and Ben was knocked sideways, feeling his shoulder smack into a post as he tumbled, quite by chance, into a large hole that he hadn't noticed until now.

It was full of cowering people.

As Ben's eyes adjusted to the light he realized that they were all soldiers and that they spoke English.

'We've got to 'old the bridge! If the Bosch get across, we're done for.'

'Keep your 'ed down Sam, you're not fighting farmers, these boys know how to shoot.'

''Scuse me?' said Ben stepping forward. Just then, someone stepped backwards, knocking him sideways; a man in a cap with a badge that looked like feathers above a sort of ribbon turned around and looked right at Ben. Or at least where Ben was lying on the ground but the man's eyes remained unfocused, as if staring right through him. The man frowned and moved on. 'Er, excuse me, what's happening, I'm English too?' Ben asked again, as he got up but either they were ignoring him or they couldn't hear him over the noise of shell-fire. It was then noticed that the men wore these strange things on their legs – bands of cloth that wrapped around their calves he'd seen in pictures and Ben also knew enough about guns to recognize that the rifles each carried were pretty old-fashioned.

'They're making a break for the bridge. Keep firing!' He looked up and in the middle distance he saw grey shapes stream down the embankment towards the canal. A volley of shots came from the dugout and several figures, no more than silhouettes in the gloom, fell, sliding down the steep bank and into the canal where they floated, face down. Ben felt sick again and very weak.

Just then, Ben got the curious sensation he was being watched. He turned and saw a small, thin soldier with odd eyes staring right at him. Ben felt uncomfortable and tried to say something but his throat constricted and no sound came out.

'Look, Charlie, there's a bleedin' kid in 'ere wiv us!'

Another soldier stopped firing and turned around. He was taller, with black hair and a thin moustache that didn't suit his heavy features. Something about the hard set of his mouth and powerful jaw reminded him of Todd's dad. 'Can't see any kid, unless you mean that messenger lad's come back.'

'No. Look!' the little soldier pointed right at Ben who

tried to lift his arm. It felt useless and leaden, like he'd fallen asleep on it for ages. His fingers tingled painfully and his whole body felt light again, as if he was back in the water. 'Oh,' Ben heard, just before he blacked out for the second time, 'that's funny – he's not there anymore – 'e must have run off...'

• • • •

He felt like he was floating again as a dark presence now carried him out of the dugout and away from the artillery fire, the explosions and the cries. Ben had the vague impression of a huge silhouette with something curious behind its back, something he could quite make out. The tall figure carried him gently away from the battle and eventually laid him down. As he stood up his arms looked webbed to his sides and Ben thought of the figure he'd seen from the coach. He seemed to have something jutting from his back, like the arch of wings. Like an angel.

• • • •

CHAPTER 10

• • • • Back

Ben woke with the morning sun warming his eyelids. He lay there for a few moments, keeping his eyes shut, feeling oddly secure.

Feeling *better*.

The tangled, utterly inexplicable events of the night before surfaced briefly in his recent memory but he pushed them aside for a few moments longer – he still needed some rest.

When he did eventually open his eyes, he found that he was lying on a patch of well-trodden grass by the canal. His clothes were damp but reasonably warm and the noise of shellfire had been replaced by the modern, reassuring swish of passing cars. There was also no sign of Todd. Nothing was threatening at all, everything seemed real and in its place. *And* in its proper time.

This, in itself, was a huge relief to Ben.

• • • •

Half an hour later, having walked back to the hotel, he'd pretty much convinced himself that what had happened after he'd hit the water was a sort of dream, that he must have fainted or lost consciousness in the canal and hallucinated. It was probably some sort of miracle he had managed to get out again.

An image of the shrouded figure surfaced and Ben's steps slowed momentarily, before he took a deep breath and forced himself not to look over his shoulder.

As he so often did – to deflect his thoughts from questions with no answer – Ben turned his attention to the strictly practical.

Right now, his immediate concern was getting into the hotel without St John realising he'd spent the night out of it. Now, that *would* be a flipping miracle. He briefly considered just sauntering up to the door and pretending he'd popped out for a walk but he dismissed the idea as really stupid: his clothes were still damp, which would be tricky to explain and it was very likely that he'd give himself away by the simple fact that no-one his age or where he was went for walks for the hell of it just before breakfast. In his experience on the estate he grew up on, people who were up before about 7am were either street cleaners or they'd woken up somewhere where they shouldn't be.

A bit like him.

He also knew that St John was out to get him on this

trip: with no other teachers, it would be his word against Ben's. It had been made clear by the Head at the start of term that he was on a last chance. If he put a foot out of place during this trip, he'd risk being expelled from the school. He may have reformed – and most of the other teachers accepted that – but St John was of the opinion he was just as bad as Todd or Banti. Worse perhaps. He was suspicious of Ben because he could not figure him out.

Ben didn't understand precisely what the problem was, but his thinking was a bit quirky, even by his own standards, which were fairly elastic thanks to living with his mum and dad for so long. The last adult to take any interest in him had been the Science and Technology teacher, Mr Cument. He put the issue of Ben's oddness this way: 'See this piece of old timber.' He waved a bit of wood under Ben's nose and then ran his finger along it. 'Cut along the grain, it is – nice and smooth. But now, look at this.' He held up another piece of identical-looking wood. 'Run your pinky along that son.' Ben shrugged and did what he was asked.

'Ow! *sir!*' Old Cument grinned.

'Got a splinter, did you?'

'Looks like it, sir.' Ben sucked his finger.

'The problem with you Bartops is you're cut at right angles, like this bit of old planking. Against the grain. Now, no one ever made life easy for themselves being all 'aphazard and rough like you – the world is made for people who run in nice simple, straight lines. You're either going to turn out to be a genius or you'll end up ...' he stopped quickly but both Ben and he knew that the rest of the sentence was going to be *end up in prison.* Like his dad. Ben thought Mr Cument was pretty much OK but he never went back to his class after that.

Ben had thought about what the old teacher had said, though, and had decided he couldn't get excited about being a genius or a loser – either way you were always going to be singled out as being an outsider, too different ... a bit abnormal. That was the big difference between him and Todd. He just wanted to be left alone for long enough to feel like he belonged.

Ben didn't know why he cared so much about staying at the school, he just knew he did. He wanted to prove everyone wrong, he guessed. But, these days, all thoughts eventually led to Ben thinking about his mum, however hard he tried to keep her separate from the one thing he had left he could control.

And being expelled would finish his mother off – Ben was seriously concerned that one day something would happen and what hadn't been chipped away of her sanity would go into hiding in her own head. And no one would ever catch a glimpse of the real her again. What little there was left of the person she once was would simply disappear as surely as if she got on a bus one day and never came back.

He cursed Todd under his breath. This was all his fault but, as usual, it was up to Ben to get himself out of a mess on his own.

• • • •

So Ben skirted around the back of the hotel, where a line of dull-looking trees attempted in a quiet, courageous way to cling on to life in a dusty courtyard. Some old garden furniture had been put there to be out of sight and mind. Ben sheltered behind the haphazardly piled plastic tables and chairs. He kept very still for a few moments, eventually spotting an open window on the first floor. A familiar arm lent across a chest of draws next to the window and fiddled with a shutter that had blown across one half of the frame.

Ben picked up a small lump of earth and chucked it at the window. It hit the glass with a much louder-than-expected bang, causing a movement from the room next door. St John's pinched, suspicious face appeared at the window. Ben's heart did a sudden panicky summersault as he ducked behind a table just in time, grimacing and screwing up his eyes. That had been too close for comfort.

When he thought it was safe to look up he spotted

Millie again. She was brushing her teeth, the clod of earth still half stuck to her window. St John had apparently disappeared from view, so Ben took a risk and dashed across the open, no-man's land of the courtyard, praying that the teacher didn't look outside again.

As soon as he got to the side of the building, he grabbed a metal drainpipe and quickly and expertly climbed up level with Millie's sill. Some things you just never forgot.

'Millie,' he hissed, almost falling as his trainer slipped off one of the drainpipe's brackets. 'Bloody hell, shit.' He turned to check his footing as the shutter was pushed open again, the sharp corner catching Ben on the forehead. This time he really did fall off, landing on the ground just as Millie's face appeared at the window, looking quizzical, and then anxious as she saw Ben sprawled on the paving stones.

'What the ...?' she just had time to mouth before St John himself stuck his own head out of his own window next door.

'Bartops!' he almost squealed, largely in delight. 'Breaking into a girl's room ... even for you that's a new low. And your clothes! Can I surmise by their state that you been for a morning swim?' Ben's heart sank to the pit of his churning stomach. This was it, then, St John finally had him ...

He was badly winded by the fall and was still fighting for breath when another voice came from a previously shut fire door.

'Zer you are!' it exclaimed as the hotel owner bustled out, picking Ben off the ground with one hand, making a show of dusting him down with a filthy dishcloth with the other. 'Break time iz over, ah need you *now*, back in zee kitchen, zis minute!'

'Wha-?' started Ben and then clamped his mouth tight shut when he saw the conspiratorial look on the Frenchman's face.

St John looked quickly at both of them, his face somehow managing to show disappointment, disbelief, and frank amazement all at the same time.

'Am I to understand, Monsieur, that *you* sent him out here?'

'Why, yes, zis little Englishman shows some talent for 'is cooking. 'E was 'elping me these morning in the keetchin, when he 'ad an, err… mis'appening with the – 'ow you say – legume, non, awh, zut …vegetable, ah oui, ze vegetable spray, it eez very temperamental, like my waif … you must warm hup immediately, I sez, or you catch def. So zis intelligent boy goes out into ma butifull garden and does 'is morning exercises … *et voila*, zis is where you find 'im.' The hotel owner turned his attention to Ben, patently ignoring St John spluttering in disbelief. 'Come inside zis eenstant, zere is work to do, if we are to 'av breakfast for my guests ready on tahm!'

• • • •

Once inside he squeezed Ben's arm. 'Not 'urt?'

Ben shook his head.

'Well, anyways, you look 'alf starving,' the owner shook his head, looking unexpectedly grave for the first time in their brief acquaintance. He cast about, then grabbed a knife and cut off a generous slice of meat from a cooked ham hanging up in an alcove,

' – take zis and some bread and go to your room and change clozzes. If you are 'ungry again, just come and see me!'

'Thanks,' said Ben, hardly daring to believe he had got away with it, 'thank you very much, um … ?'

'Ma name iz Bertrand, but you can coll me Plastic – long storee.'

He winked heavily at Ben.

And Ben, feeling utterly grateful, escaped before he embarrassed himself.

• • • •

CHAPTER 11

· · · · Banti

Half an hour later, back in some dry clothes, Ben now walked as casually as possible into the dining room at the hotel. Bertrand (who seemed to be the only person who actually worked there) looked over from where he was serving Mr. St John a pot of coffee. Keeping his face blank, the Frenchman cocked an eyebrow at Ben before bustling back into the kitchen through some swing doors.

With a sinking feeling, Ben noticed Todd from the other side of the room looking at him strangely, probably trying to work out what had happened the night before. Ben was frankly still as mystified as his former friend. Banti, who had almost certainly already heard what had happened between the two of them, scowled and made a slit-throat gesture at Ben who ignored him and went over to a dark corner and sat by himself.

The self-enforced isolation didn't last long – after a few moments Millie picked up her half-eaten toast and her orange juice and came over.

'Mind if I sit here?' she asked cheerfully, and sat down without waiting for an answer.

'Gmmuffin,' Ben replied through a mouthful of pastry that had just expanded to twice its size the second Millie looked at him with her hazel eyes. She grinned lopsidedly.

'Wow, smooth talker,' out of the corner of his eye, he noticed Lucy Pint and Zac whisper and giggle as they looked over at Ben and Millie. 'Have you recovered from your circus clowning this morning?'

'Just about … it only hurts when I try and do anything mad – like move or breath.'

'What on Earth were you up to? St John nearly caught you and, worse still, you might have broken your neck.' Ben thought about making something up and then decided he couldn't be bothered. It was only 9am but it had already been a long day.

'I was trying to get into your room.' Millie's eyes opened wide in outraged.

'Bloody cheek!'

Ben panicked. 'No, no, it's not like that!' which, of course, just made it sound worse. Millie's eyes narrowed dangerously – she may have been in the Year 10 but she was almost Ben's age and technically she was quite scary. He talked fast. 'I'd been out all night and St John couldn't find out, so I was trying to sneak in the back way. I'll get kicked out if I get caught so much as thinking about breaking a single school rule until I leave.'

'*Outallnightareyoutotallyoffyourrockcer?*'

Toast went everywhere plus it came out louder than she meant it to. Instinctively, they both turned to see if St John had heard anything. Luckily, he seemed engrossed in a guidebook.

'Not by choice, take my word for it.' But before he had a chance to go any further there was a movement from behind Ben as Banti pushed past and planted himself on the lip of the table, knocking over a bowl of sugar in the process. Ignoring Ben, he stuck his hand out to Millie.

'Enchanted, my name's Banti – Bartholomew … to the ladies.' Millie just glared at him.

'Well that's hardly my fault.' Ben saw that St John had now finished breakfast and was preparing to leave the room. There were no other adults about and Todd seemed to be watching the scene from a distance with a sort of close detachment.

Banti slid off the tabletop and sat next to Ben, putting an arm that felt like a lump of dead meat around his shoulders. He ruffled Ben's hair, forcing his head this way and that. As his temple still ached from the accident, Ben winced. 'You've been saying things about me, apparently. Things which ain't very friendly. And I don't remember givin' you permission to talk about me … ' He broke off and glared at Ben who simply sat and stared at his huge classmate, 'so I thought I'd come over here an' ask for an apology.' He stuck out a fat hand. Ben noticed it already had hair growing on the back of his knuckles. 'That'll be fifty quid, you owe me for hurtin' my feelins. And I'll be havin' a tenner off you every month by way of a reminder.'

Ben glanced at Banti's hand shrugged and picked up his toast. Like all career bullies, Banti Croft had several forms of attack – without any visible effort, he moved up a gear.

'How's your mum, by the way?' He said this very loudly, so everyone could hear. Most of the kids at school knew about Mrs. Bartops but no one had dared mention her before. There was another long pause whilst it sunk in that a line had been crossed. Millie shifted in her seat but Ben carried on calmly eating his toast. When it became clear he wasn't going to answer, Banti lent over and flicked Ben's hot cocoa, tipping it down Ben's trousers. It wasn't hot anymore, which was something he supposed he should be grateful for. Ben looked up quickly and met Millie's eye. He shook his head, as if to say, *don't do anything*.

Seeing he still wasn't getting a reaction seemed to make Banti even angrier. 'Is your mum still mad? Does she dribble? My granny used to dribble a lot *and* she stank. I bet your mum stinks too, I bet she needs a nappy –'

But Banti was suddenly unable to continue.

Ben moved fast: he wrenched the bottom of Banti's t-shirt in one practiced movement, pulling the back up over his head. Then, grabbing a bottle of brown sauce from the table, he squeezed the contents down the back of Banti's trousers, who roared in anger and stood up. Unfortunately for him he couldn't move his arms to steady himself or see anything either and no sooner had he stood up then he fell over a chair. Ben kicked him hard and satisfyingly in the ribs. He was still sprawling on the floor, his trousers a mess, and his shirt over his head when St John came running in. 'Gentlemen, gentle*men*! What's happening, here? I demand an explanation!'

Millie smiled sweetly at him. 'Croft's had a bit of a, um ... *personal* accident sir, if you get my drift. It's not his fault and the least said soonest mended as my nana ways says, but I think he needs to go to his room and change.' Banti may have been feared but he wasn't in the least popular and the rest of the pupils allowed themselves barely stifled laughter – something they would never normally have dared. Banti had just lost against Ben – a boy half his size – and it would take him a long time to get that respect back, if he ever did. Everyone who had ever suffered from Banti's bullying allowed themselves a small public celebration.

St John stared around the room, his eyes scanning this way and that, moving over the laughing students.

His eye eventually rested on Ben who had fortunately had the good sense to move quickly to another table as far away from the action as possible. Ben took a thoughtful sip of orange juice and did his best to look entirely innocent.

'Yes, well,' said St John eventually, 'Croft, I don't care to think about what that is all over the back of your trousers but you better *had* change. The rest of you can tidy this mess up and be ready in the car park in fifteen minutes, we've got a museum visit planned this morning – God help me.'

St John left the room to a mixture of subsiding laughter and groans. They had all assumed they'd get another free day.

With everyone otherwise engaged, Ben watched warily as Todd now slid out of his chair and sauntered over to where Ben was sitting. 'Now I don't know where you vanished to last night … even thought you'd drowned, he nodded in Banti's direction. 'Rules ov the games is changin' mon, weez not iccle kids no more …' he paused long enough to change persona again. He stared coldly at Ben. 'Just try something like that with me … see what I do to you…'

Ben looked at Todd for a long time without saying anything. 'I won't fight you Todd.' He said it so matter-of-factly that Todd looked briefly confused, then he re-grouped.

'The thing about Banti,' he remarked almost conversationally, 'is 'e's stupid but 'e just keeps going. 'Ee's done fings – stone cold sober mind, not 'amstered – fings make your 'air stand on end. He'll be after you again … and when he eventually gets those dirty great hands of 'is on you, you better hope you end up back in 'ospital, if not, then I reckon we'll finish our little chat. And it'll be worse than a few bumps and bruises.'

• • • •

CHAPTER 12

• • • • Man in the photograph

'Sir, is it true that the Germans killed a load of kids like us, Sir?'

St John rolled his eyes and sighed at something far above his head. They were standing inside the museum looking at a large yellowing board which had four columns, each in a different language, all describing the same thing – **The Battle of Mons: 23-24 August 1914**!! The bit written in English didn't sound quite right but it was more interesting than listening to their teacher:

> The German army, according to the rules of the plan called Schliefflen, were now advancing with great haste towards the city of Paris. In France. The French army had been slaughtered with many loss of life further in the south and so the English commander of the British Expeditionary Force (called 'Old Contemptibles' by the German Kaiser), General Sir John French, was strongly depressed to find his small force of 70,000 men unexpectedly faced with the main attacking of the entire German army who was in a big hurry to leave Belgium.

> Sir John agreed to hold fast his position for one
> day and what followed was the Battle for Mons.

'Sir, is it true the Germans used gas on us in the war!'

'I'll use gas on you in a minute Stelco, if you don't keep quiet and read.'

'Sir, that's intimidation, Sir!' Mr St John sighed again.

'Look Stelco, I appreciate that for once in your stop-start school career, the Great War and all it's carnage is a subject you appear to have an aptitude for. However, whilst there were reported atrocities carried out on civilians and even nuns in Belgium, these could well have been exaggerated to get the Catholic Irish to fight for the British … and, whilst it is true that the Germans were the first to use gas against the British in the trenches, the British had, in fact, used gas themselves – rather liberally – against the Boers in South Africa. There are few innocent parties in war, especially a war like this one.'

At this Todd, muttering darkly to himself, disappeared off to the museum shop, leaving Ben and the rest of them to carry on reading:

> Early on the morning of 23rd August, the first
> British shots of the war were fired by a small force
> in Casteau, up on the hill above Mons. The fighting
> very quickly intensed as the British retreated to the

canal where they kept the much larger German army from crossing and gaining the road to Paris.

However, after many blessed casualties, on 24th the British were forced to flee away from the canal. An UNKNOWN SOLDIER from the Middlesex Regiment covered their retreat at Obourg Station, saving his friends. His identity was never verified and the brave man most probably died in the station itself.

The situation was still very grave …

HOWEVER, just when all seemed lost, there then came reports of a GHOSTLY APPARITION – some say an angel, others claim it was IN FACT the ghost of an archer from the battle of Azincourt. This phantom rose up in front of the advancing Germans, striking terror into their ranks and so the small British Force were rescued!

Today the existence of the angel or archer (most popularly known as the Angel of Mons) is poo poo'ed by experts but there are many confirmed reports of sightings on that day and others in August. More strangely still, many of the German casualties were reported to have ARROW wounds when they were brought off the field of battle ….

Something in Ben's mind seemed to go click and his arms suddenly felt tingly and weirdly disconnected from the rest of his body. And he knew why.

At the edge of the board there was a picture of a group of British soldiers, smoking away, grinning gamely at the camera. Their uniforms looked the same as the ones he'd seen himself in the fighting the night before. It had been dark but flashes of light from the heavy artillery had given him glimpses of gaiters, cloth caps and boots that matched *exactly* what he saw now in the antique picture. Ben stepped away from the board, almost falling as he bumped into Zac.

'Watch out!'

'Sorry ... er, Zac' said Ben vaguely. He moved outside, pressing his hands to his temples. Perhaps it was the accident, perhaps he'd banged his head harder than anyone had suspected. He thought about going back to the hospital and looking for the tired lady doctor with the down-turned mouth but caring eyes.

Ben sat down heavily on the cool stone steps. More than anything, he was suddenly scared by the thought that what was happening to him had something to do with his mother's illness. Perhaps it could be inherited and now it was coming out as these weird visions of things that had happened here nearly a hundred years before.

Ben shuddered at another recollection; as he had

staggered away from the photo inside the museum, he'd seen a blurred outline, cloaked and black, standing some way off in the background of the picture. To anyone else, it probably looked like a smudge or some dirt on the lens but Ben recognized it instantly. He knew, beyond any doubt, that it was the same figure he'd seen by the motorway two days ago and then by the canal.

The cloaked man who had saluted him as the bus had crashed.

• • • •

CHAPTER 13

Third Man Theory

A couple of hours later they were sat on the cobbles in the main square, stuffing their faces with McDonalds. All except Ben – who didn't really mind. First up, thanks to Bertrand, he'd eaten more that morning than he usually did in a whole day and, secondly, he'd taken some bread, dried sausage and a bottle of water from the hotel to keep himself from getting too hungry or thirsty during the day. To last him the next couple of days, he still had a blue, five euro note, which reminded him of toy money, but he was saving that for an emergency.

In any case, he'd lost his appetite back at the museum.

Ben sat apart from the group and listened to Todd lecture everyone about the various weapons used in the First World War, the benefits and weaknesses and, most importantly, what they would do to you.

'The Brits 'ad your Lee Enfield – you could kill a man over half a mile away and if someone was standing behind him, the bullet would go right through the first bloke and kill the second stone dead. There isn't anyfing even half as accurate around today … it's all *ba ba ba ba*, spraying bullets everywhere as if they're gangstas, no *finesse* my dad says. It weren't no machine gun but it could fire so quick that the Germans thought we all had Maxim guns ... oh yeah, now Maxim guns were the best machine guns in the war – they 'ardly ever jammed and they could fire 600 rounds a minute. When they was invented everyone said that there would be no more war 'cos they killed so many soldiers, shot down in their millions, that no-one would want to fight anymore ... didn't work though and they said the same fing about nuclear bombs in the Second World War but people still have a go at each other, bloody typical ... Anyway where was I ... that's right, guns ... the officers all carried pistols at the start but they soon stopped 'cos they were useless unless you got really close and the Germans used to aim at the bloke up at the front carrying the pistol, 'cos if they shot an officer they got a pat on the back and maybe extra booze ...'

Even Millie was listening intently. Todd paused and took a huge slurp of coke, burped noisily and continued.

'... but it wasn't just guns, everyone invented loads of cool stuff during the war just to get the upper hand on the enemy. Like your grenade. At the start of the war everyone used home made grenades made out of jam jars they stuffed with explosives and bits of metal they found lyin' about. Bit primitive but better than the ones they got from the government that were like as not going to blow up in your 'and before you got a chance to chuck it at the enemy. Blow 'alf your face off they would … you might stay alive for days, dying slowly in agony, screaming …'

'Oh yuk, do we have to listen to this?' Lucy Pint pulled a face but she stayed put. Todd knew a weakness when he heard it. He grinned evilly.

'That wasn't the worst; there was flame throwers that shot petrol out of a hose, right across this square they could go, and barbeque anyfing in sight. Men turned into charred statues where they stood. Clear out a trench full of men quicker than you could say *shish kebab*. An' worst of all mustard gas. Even one whiff and you wouldn't stop coughing again until the day you died. Get a lungful of the stuff and it was like you'd just swallowed boiling tar. The gas would burn your eyes in their sockets, too.'

'That's it, does anyone want the rest of my burger?' Banti had gone pale green.

'Ooh ta mate,' said Todd cheerfully, making a grab for it, like he'd won a prize, 'don't mind if I do.'

• • • •

Ben zoned out, retreating back to his troubled thoughts about mysterious figures, hallucinations and the very real chance he stood of going mad. He was surprised, then, when Zac leaned over and offered Ben the rest of his chips. 'Cheers Zac,' he said, taking one, 'sorry about barging into you earlier.'

'Don't mention it. You seemed a bit upset by something back there.'

'Yeah, um I got a bit hot and that stuff about the angel freaked me out.' Ben kept his head down, concentrating on the chips. When he looked up he saw that Zac was staring at him in a strange way. 'What?'

'That stuff about the angel ...' said Zac.

Ben remembered something about Zac's dad teaching in the local church on Sundays. 'Yeah, what about it?'

'It's true you know.'

Ben shook his head, forcing a grin. 'Are you sure you've just got coke in there? I noticed they serve beer in McDonalds out here.'

'No seriously – loads of people seen it and not just in the First World War. Climbers and people who walk about across glaciers an' the like, they've even got a name for it.' Despite himself, Ben was interested.

'What's that then?'

'*Third Man Theory*. Lots of people, normal people near death, stuck out in the freezing snow or lost up mountains have said that they were guided home by a stranger who appeared at their side – a ghostly figure that led them to safety, never uttering a single word but always staying with them, showing the way, giving them comfort. Like an angel – you know – a guardian angel.'

• • • •

CHAPTER 14

Extract from the journal of Corporal Sam
Lyle, 4th Middlesex Regiment. • • • • • •

22nd August 1914, Mons, Belgium.

First the Indian Uprising, then three years chasing
the Boers across those huge plains out there that went
on to eternity; miserable, hot months, rounding up their
families, burning their farms, poor sods, and now all this
right on our doorstep. It seems like all me and Charlie
have done since signing up all those years ago on the
Old Kent Road just as kids really is sat on ships
waiting to be taken to some foreign spot to shoot
at a crowd of other human beings we've never met
and, truth be told, don't have anything much against.
Seventeen years of service and all I'll get is a
corporal's pension, even if I make it that far,
and a hundred nasty memories I can't stop thinking
about if I tried. But I'll do my duty.

We'd spent the whole of the following day after the
skirmish at Casteau down by the canal, digging
ourselves in. It kept our minds off all the Germans

we'd seen massing up on the hill.

Our platoon have been making a sort of dugout, chipping away at the rock-hard earth, until we had this dirty great hole with half a dozen firing posts and shelter – thanks to sandbags – where a man could sleep if he had the chance. Or lie down to die.

A British soldier likes nothing more than cleaning his gun or digging an hole (so says Charlie) and he's right – morale is high enough amongst the men but the officers appear to be out of sorts. Sergeant Trisk explained it to us as we dug that they're not happy about having to fight here. "Fact is this canal is the best defence for miles but it's pretty useless all the same. I can see half a dozen bridges just looking one way. I don't know how we're going to stop them getting across."

"Can we just blow em up, Sarge?" Well, old Trisk knocked his pipe against a railway sleeper we was using as a footstep and shook his head.

"I thought of that but the Frenchies won't let us, it'll destroy the canal – a lot of these bridges are attached to locks. They might need the canal later."

"Can't go boating if you're dead Sarge."

"True, private, true. But ours is not to reason why and it still doesn't change the fact we shouldn't be fighting in this town. I don't know who was more surprised – the Bosch when they bumped into the entire British army ... or us."

"How do you know they weren't waiting for us?"
That was Sid. The Sergeant glared a bit at him.

"They're professionals. If they knew we was coming we'd've had a bit more of a welcoming party and no time to dig ourselves in down 'ere. So make the most of it!" he suddenly raises his voice at us, "and let's get this thing finished before dark — they could come at any moment!"

And come they did....

Dusk was falling — a dark grey blanket that started in the East and drew itself across the sky like a cover. Not so much of lick of red in the sun, which spelled rain the next day. A few of the men started to make up evening brews and cook a bit of dinner.

It all seemed like spot of camping after a hard day's work and someone even suggested a late game of soccer.

But just then a machine gunner opened up to the left of our position, sweeping covering fire across our positions. It made a different noise to our own Maxim — caca'caca'ca — almost like it was coughing bullets down the slope where we crouched, keeping our heads down. Another of their gunners opened in the centre, which was immediately answered by one on the far right.

Everyone ran for cover, although I noticed a few of our chaps fall before they got to their shallow defences. Heavy machine gun rounds hit some railway tracks in a cascade of sparks and richoche'ed off them — one round buzzing past my left ear.

No-one was relaxed and happy anymore.

I risked a peek between the metal tracks and straightaways wished I hadn't bothered.

You know, there's always a bit in them books I used to read to you before we turned the lights out — the ones where brave Brits go out and tame foreign lands single-handed, or Americans coves win the West and the hero always gets the girl — the bits I'm talking about are usually near the end when he looks out across a plain and sees thousands of natives charging at him, waving spears, shouting about something or other and there's no way out for our hero.

This was just like that bit in the flicks then, except these was heavily armed Germans! Swarms of them, sweeping down the slope towards our positions and we was the real world, the one where miracles don't happen. You just get shot and buried in the corner of some foreign field, like poor Parr earlier.

"You've gone a bit pale, Sam. Where the 'ells our gunners gawn?" asks Charlie, "bout time we got some artillery pieces up 'ere an all." He takes a quick peek at the German positions, same as I did, and his face seems to sag, like he's had a stroke. "Oh my Lord and saints," Charlie's hands shake like an old man's as he tried to light a fag. "We'll not live to see another day." He whispers so only I can hear. "There's ten of 'em for every one of us and more arriving by the bleedin' minute by the looks of it."

But, just then, our own gunners opened up and a ragged cheer ran along our lines as silhouettes of German soldiers in the middle distance tumbled and fell. We still had our firepower, even if we was desperate for more men.

And so it had started.

The rest of the night and most of the next day was one long drawn out barrage of mayhem, the like none of us experienced soldiers had ever seen or dreamt of. A desperate effort to hold our positions. If we had to fall back, away from the canal, we'd be overwhelmed and die. We had to stay and accept our fate.

Just after it got properly dark a strange thing did happen. We was visited by a ghost in our little dugout.

I saw him first, maybe 'cos he was looking right at me. He looked frightened by all the noise, which is odd … for a ghost. His mouth moved but no sound came out. At first I thought he was a local lad, about ten years old I'd say, who'd got lost somehow between the lines and ended up crawling into the first bit shelter he could find. But that didn't seem right, somehow. He was standing no more than two feet away from me, but he didn't seem to fit in — it was like he had been painted onto the scene, like they do in the movies, or in the theatre — he looked like a backdrop.

Then he vanished from right under my nose.

. . . .

CHAPTER 15

• • • • Ghost story

In spite of the quiet panic over what seemed to be happening to him, Ben actually began to feel sleepy in the afternoon sunlight that still poured into the town square over the tops of the buildings. His classmates' voices gradually faded into the background – gruesome facts about weaponry from Todd had given way to nerve-jangling stories of ghostly apparitions, thanks to Zac, and the rest of them were competing to go one better than each other in a succession of unlikely tales and spectres.

Ben had always been more scared than he would have cared to admit by ghost stories at the best of times but the shadowy robed figure, who now seemed to be following him around Belgium, had made him lose his taste for that sort of thing altogether. The idea of having a guardian angel was supposed to be all cosy and comforting but this dark man who turned up in moments of danger had something almost sinister about him: a brooding sense of unpredictability – and Ben knew all about that. He also just didn't buy the *all-angels-have-got-to-be-good* angle. Over ninety years ago, Ben's new companion had apparently killed German soldiers – they may well have been the enemy but who was he to take sides? He had *perhaps* pulled Ben from the water and carried him away from the fighting but he had also calmly watched the coach crash. Ben had the vague, disturbing feeling that whoever or perhaps whatever he was, he was just as capable taking away life as saving it.

'That one was so boring it's probably true,' remarked Todd dismissively, making Millie blush. She'd just finished an unconvincing story about a ghost bus that drove through London on rainy nights.

'Did it run people over?' asked Lucy trying to be supportive.

'Er, no, I don't think so.'

'Like I said, B-O-R-I-N-G. But I know a good one and it's true 'cos it 'appened to me Auntie and Uncle just last year. We all went around the next day and they told us it straight off. My Aunt's hair went completely white that very night, even 'er eyebrows. '

'OK, then,' said Millie who was still annoyed about what Todd had just said about her story, 'let's hear it then.'

'Alright, I will,' he said confidently, 'but first let me tell you a bit about my Uncle Vernon. First fing you need to know is 'e's an Undertaker. Point bein', he works wif death, knows it like you or I know the living.

Uncle Vernon's tall and thin and 'e never, ever smiles.' Todd looked thoughtful. 'Leastways not now ... not anymore ... not after what happened in their house.'

'Go on,' said Banti, his mouth slack.

'Useful to 'av an undertaker in the family, never know when you might need to get rid of a body ... ' said Todd, still musing ' ... anyway, where was I, oh, yeah ... the house – well, they lived on the edge of a cemetery, dead creepy it was, even in summer an' their house was tall and thin, wif the mortuary – the place where they kept the corpses – in the basement which they kept freezin' cold all year round on account of the bodies starting to smell what with the central heating an' all ...

'Anyway, one night Auntie Kay and Vernon had been out for a few drinks and a bite 'an they come back to the house. All dark it is an' the only noise is the fridge humming in the mortuary and the wind moanin' in the dead trees surrounding their house like Dementers. Vernon lets them in the back door that leads down some steps to the basement as 'e likes to 'av a look around before going to bed.

''E doesn't bovver turning the lights on or nuffink, 'cos there's always a bit of light from the street outside, pouring in through the long windows at the end, lighting up the white sheets with dead people lying cold on metal trolleys, some with toes sticking out the end, all bloodless an' blue – seen it meself – dozens of times. Everyfing seems to be OK, so they make themselves a cup of tea and go upstairs.

'But 'ere's the fing …

'No sooner 'as my auntie started to get ready f'bed when there's a terrible screaming … coming from downstairs. "Get away from me!" this girl is crying at the top of her lungs, "get away, leave me … leave me alone … *pleeaase!*" In the darkness the whole of the house is shakin' with the noise of her terrible screams. And this is not just any girl, bof my Auntie and Uncle look at each other in 'orror. "Sal," they say at the same moment. "Our little Sal." Cos it's her voice, they are hearing coming from their basement …

'the terrified screams of their only daughter. My cousin.

"But Sal's not 'ere," says my auntie, "she's on 'er 'olidays."

'So, of course, when they get back downstairs there is nobody there, just the corpses but there's still the screaming and by now bof are half mad wiv bein' frantic and the terror of it. They look this way an' that and pinpoint the sound – and it's coming from one of the new bodies wot's all zipped up. My uncle runs over and then hesitates, 'is 'ands shakin as he fiddles with the zipper. *It's 'er, 'e finks to 'imself, I'm goin' to find my darling daughter in this bag.* An' still the screaming goes on, my aunt falls to the floor, holding her ears to drown it out.

'Finally 'e gets the zipper undone just as the cries stop.

'There's total silence now in the mortuary as they both look at the corpse of this dried-up old man, 'is mouth all puckered and tight, where 'is false teef 'av been removed but the strange fing is is 'is jaw is still movin' but no sound is coming out anymore, like 'e's run out of air in 'is dead lungs.

' "It's not her," says my aunt eventually, looking relieved. "Oh Vernon, thank God it's not our baby!"

'But Uncle Vernon's not convinced. "That might not be 'er body but it was 'er voice."

' "But she's not even 'ere. She's in America, you know that."

'An' Vernon was right and all. The next day they found out she'd been murdered. By some maniac – strangled 'er to def....'

There was a long silence.

'You're full of crap,' said Millie but no-one, not even Ben, believed that Todd was telling anything but the complete and utter truth.

• • • •

CHAPTER 16

. . . . Again

Ben knew that Todd wasn't bluffing – he didn't have to. If he found himself alone with Banti or Todd they'd hurt him. Badly if they could. So when they all decided it was time to go back to the hotel, Ben made a show of leaving with them all but then quietly slipped off, down the first side alley they passed.

He certainly wasn't about to risk going back to the hotel right away; instead, he found himself drifting out of town once again, instinctively moving towards a set of stubbly fields, newly harvested at the end of the summer that seemed to stretch the horizon in every direction, away from the canal. He was lost in thought, hardly noticing his surroundings, even as it got dark and started to rain. Slowly, inexorably, his feet led him away from the noise of traffic and people and into open countryside.

After some time, a waft of acrid smoke made him look up. He stared out across the stubbled, utterly flat countryside with its broad fields, bordered with dark trees. Although it hadn't rained for weeks, this landscape was somehow dotted with shallow lakes that lay on the surface of the sodden mud reflecting the grey skies – like pools of mercury.

Then *the real* seemed to shift ever so slightly; afterwards it was hard to describe but at first it appeared to Ben as if the wind simply changed direction – and yet, when Ben looked about him once more, the monochrome landscape was no longer *precisely* the same – the trees were not the ones that had been there just moments earlier, and the pools of water now reflected quite different clouds.

It was happening again.

Ben realised he had just left where he once was, and now stood in the ghost of a countryside it had once been.

But this time he knew what he had to do: he turned and started to walk in the gathering gloom towards where his instinct told him the dugout lay.

• • • •

Once he got there, the land around the battle lines was pitch dark, as if it were no longer early evening but closer to midnight. Then, without preamble, the guns resumed their firing. But it was intermittent, with none of the hysteria and sense of madness from his first visit.

As Ben reached the dugout he saw soldiers lying in shallow hollows, wrapped in ground sheets trying to sleep. A candle lit up a corrugated corner where the soldier – the one who had recognized him from the night before – wrote in a tattered book as the rain came down. Ben stood for a time and watched the small corporal writing away, wondering why he was there and thinking about what had happened in the last few days. He looked at the cover of the notebook.

Timothy 'Sam' Lyle

it said, in neat copperplate,

21 Fludd St, London.

Ben knew the road – it was no more than a mile from where he used to live on the estate.

Ben sat down, his chin resting on his bent knees to keep out the cold, which gradually seeped through his already damp clothes as the minutes turned to hours. He sat for a very long time, feeling sure the reason for these visits would come to him, knowing in his heart what was happening could not be an accident. Then, over the sound of artillery, he heard someone crying further along the trench. Moving silently, he came to a small bundle of khaki.

A boy, not much older than him, lay in the mud, his head pressed in his hands, sobs shaking his body. But as Ben stretched out to comfort him, the phantom scene melted away.

• • • •

CHAPTER 17

23rd August 1914, evening, Mons, Belgium.

Young Tommy Heater got back to the bunker after the worst of the fighting was over.

Poor little mite, though — he's too young and he's taken the first furious shelling very hard — can't stop shaking and crying, can't help hisself, even when Charlie growled at him to put a sock in it.

Charlie looks a bit worse for wear too — grey, silent most of the time, smoking one fag after another. He was at the end of his tether after the last fighting in Africa, so I can only imagine what this is doing to him. He's not a coward, he just can't bear feeling trapped, and this muddy hole we're in is beginning to feel more like a tomb with every passing hour.

Can't say I blame him — all these years a professional soldier and I never seen an attack like that what we saw today. Tens of thousands, all trying to cross the canal at once — us throwing everything we got at them — them throwing the same, and a lot more, besides, back.

It's how I imagine Hell is.

The Little Ghost was back again in the night. I still don't know why he's here, I can't help feeling it means something but what I cannot say. Leastways, not yet.

Anyway, he's just a lad. It's funny he doesn't dress like us, his shoes look queer – like white, springy slippers and his coat's a big quilt – I wouldn't mind something like that meself, when the weather starts to turn. His face looks familiar though – bone thin and his eyes are knowing – older than the rest of 'im. Bit like any of the kids around our way, the ones you see hanging about on corners, avoiding your eye and somehow measuring you up at the same time.

Listen to me – banging on about ghosts and complaining about the war. I know if I was to send this to you it would get chopped and crossed with that black marker pen the Lieutenant uses on all the other lads' letters – I seen him. So I think I'll wait and give it to you meself. That way I can chatter on as much as I like but I know you'll read every word when we're in front of the fire listening to the wireless and I'm having a quiet kip. So it can wait until when I next see you. If ever I do. Sorry, I didn't mean that. I AM coming back. I'd like the chance to be a better husband, a better father ... there, at home.

It's getting light now and it's stopped raining, finally. The sun's coming up, all red and sore-looking, like a great eye that's been weeping through the night.

. . . .

CHAPTER 18

• • • • Wrong

Ben woke up slowly to a livid sky. He had walked back to the hotel after the Dugout had faded to find everyone already in their rooms and probably fast asleep. It was the first time in days that he'd slept in a proper bed and he meant to make the most of it.

He turned over.

The smell of dry, clean linen opened a door in his head and a memory stole in ...

• • • •

It was early spring but to Ben it was like the first day the world had been created. He was five and his dad was taking him swimming, then they were going to McDonald's for a Happy Meal, with a Star Wars toy, he'd seen it on TV, then they were going to the river, to *their* boat. His dad had made the boat from a kit he'd ordered off the Internet on his brand new laptop and Ben had helped with some of the gluing, which was really hard but Dad made it easy by showing him how.

Their boat was red and it was called *Ranger*, Ben had chosen the name and the colour, because Power Rangers were really awesome. Just like Star Wars.

That morning, sunlight found a way in through the gaps in the curtains and he was thinking about getting up but then his dad came, so he pretended to be asleep still. Dad sort of shook and cuddled him at the same time and Ben wriggled deeper into the soft duvet that smelled of cosy things.

• • • •

At swimming, Dad let Ben wear the locker key around his wrist, just like a Ben 10 watch. He got cross when Ben ran off but he'd only gone to say hi to his friend Evan who was six and even though he lived in a flat too, he had a dog called George, with metal on its collar. But it was OK, he wasn't cross for long because then they went on the hippo slide and Dad let him ride on his shoulders when the wave machine started.

At McDonalds they'd run out of Luke Skywalker and so the man gave Ben Obi-Wan Kenobe who also had a light sabre but his was blue. Ben had really wanted Luke Skywalker or a storm trooper but he didn't say anything. His dad could put a whole hamburger in his mouth at once.

Then they went down to the river where the boat was

and the water looked grey and wavy, a bit like the sea. But Ben wasn't scared for long because although it was really windy, they went really fast, so fast it was a bit hard to breath and laugh at the same time and Dad laughed too, proper laughing like grown ups don't really do unless they're watching TV or in the pub for ages and ages.

When they got home, the policemen were already there.

Ben started to cry when they made his dad get in the car and then he dropped Obi-Wan Kenobe in the gutter trying to run his fastest down the road … trying to get his dad back.

• • • •

Later that morning, Ben used two of his five remaining euros to buy a phone card. Last day, he thought, and he better let his mum know that he was alright and coming home soon.

He didn't feel alright though. He felt confused and, at the same time, he couldn't stop thinking about the soldier who he was now sure could see him and the boy he'd come across crying in the Dugout – the scared, under fed scrap of a kid in an outsized khaki uniform who could have been in the same year as Ben at school. Strangely, they felt more real to him than his classmates at breakfast that morning. He had barely made it through the meal – his head felt heavy and light at the same time and everyone around him sounded like they were talking under water.

But absolutely everything felt more real than the dislocated, dreamy voice of his mother when she picked up the phone. '*Hiiiiiiiiii.*'

'Mum?'

Silence.

'Hi Mum, it's me.'

More silence.

Then a sort of sigh or, at least, a barely audible exhalation.

'Benny?' Her voice sounded small. *Frightened Mum* today, then.

Somewhere in one of the cupboards, perhaps the one next to the settee, there was an old-fashioned video. On the front was a faded TDK/BBC sticker with some writing. *Noel Edmunds presents, Amazing Kids! 1982*, it said. *Clare Peek, Mathmagician, aged 12.* They still had a dusty VHS cassette player under the telly with a peeling 'Wham!' sticker on it. Sometimes Ben thought that the only reason for keeping the video recorder was that cassette. He had come to hate that stupid video but he used to love it. He hated it precisely because it showed how far downhill his mum had gone. How she used to be. In 1982 she'd been famous for a bit. *The kid who could do sums quicker than a calculator.*

His mum, on the other hand, still loved it. He'd come home some days from school to find her watching the old recording. If she knew the answers to the questions now, then it was only because she had the whole thing memorised. This morning, however, Ben doubted she knew the day of the week, let alone the square root of 345.

'How are you Mum?'

There was another exhalation, this time sharper and Ben felt the atmosphere change, as surely as if he had been standing in the room with her and it had suddenly started to drizzle.

'What do you care?' You've just abandoned me … dancing off on your holidays with your little friends …

'

• • • •

Don't rise to it, the local GP had told him once, just agree and move on to a more constructive part of the conversation.

Did that psychiatrist even *know* his mum? Ben had thought at the time. Changing the subject with her was like trying to herd cats.

She must have been standing in the kitchen because he heard something slide off a surface and break on the bare concrete floor. The council hadn't got around to putting the lino down yet. The sudden crash down the receiver made Ben jump and instantly his insides knotted up. This was going to be a bad one.

When her voice came on the line again, she was someone else, a person a million miles away from the bright young thing who answered Noel's questions with a confident smile, ' ... running after your mates as usual, like a little puppy, leaving me to worry myself sick.'

'Mum, I told you, we had an accident, we've been waiting for another bus ...' but he knew it was pointless.

'Don't lie to ME!' her voice was almost a shriek now and suddenly Ben just wanted to drop the phone and run out of the box, in order to get as far away from it as possible. He had a feeling that even if he did, somehow her voice would still follow him down the road, screaming, tinny but very audible as he fled. So he stayed.

'We're going home this evening,' he said as calmly as possible, keeping his tone neutral. 'I'll be home before you wake up. I'll make you breakfast in bed!' Another sharp crash as something else broke.

'Make me breakfast ... with WHAT? Stale bread, some half-rotted bananas, a bottle of cooking sherry from Christmas ten years ago ... that's all there is! DO YOU THINK I HAVE HAD TIME, WITH EVERY-

THING ELSE I'VE GOT TO DO, TO GO SHOPPING FOR YOU,' Ben pressed the receiver to his pounding head and sank to his knees. He was aware that she was now sobbing between screams, incoherent, but he ceased listening to the words themselves anyway, they had become a jumble, as hard to fathom as her personality itself. ' ... YOU THOUGHTLESS, UNGRATEFUL, PIECE OF SHIT YOU'RE NOT MY SON ... .'

He wouldn't cry, not this time ... not ever again ... he made a pact with himself but, despite everything, the words came out anyway. '*Mummy*, please ...'

'Oh *Mummy* now is it? Think you can run off, just do what you like and then call on me when you need something. Well that's not how life is ... this is reality, you're born on your own, you'll die alone and in between you have to learn to stand on your own two feet. So don't you *mummy wummy* me!'

Ben had screwed his eyes up, so he didn't see the figure behind him. So wrapped up in his misery that he didn't notice anything until he felt Banti's fist hit the side of his head. As Ben started to fall sideways with the force of it, Banti's knee connected to his stomach, knocking all the wind out of him. Oddly, his first thought was to try and get the receiver back onto its cradle, so his mother wouldn't have to hear what was happening. He reached up to do so but Banti grabbed his wrist hard and twisted the phone out of his hand.

'Say *bye bye* to your son, Misses Mad Lady – he's *dead!*' he shouted down the receiver before putting it down on a shelf, carefully making sure the connection wasn't cut.

'Ben, Ben?' was all he heard as Banti went to work on Ben's ribs with his feet. At least his mother had stopped shouting now, was Ben's last coherent thought as he cradled his head and waited for the beating to end.

• • • •

Banti must have got tired after a minute or two because the kicks became less powerful and eventually petered out. Ben had witnessed enough violence to know that this didn't mean he could take his hands away from his head and look up. He'd seen enough kids on the estate get one last blow to the head that way, just before the attackers ran off. It was usually this one – the parting shot – that did the real damage.

In the end someone started to prise his fingers away from his face for him. He looked up. It was Todd. No sign of Banti. This was worse and Ben knew whatever he did next would have to count.

'Oh Ben,' said Todd in mock concern. 'What 'orrible little savage did this to you? I tell you, you're a constant source of vaxation n' worry to me Ben

Bartops – jumpin' in canals, getting smashed up in buses – you need protectin'. You just start doin' what you're told and leave the rest to me. Nuffin' like this will ever happen to you again … '

'Todd.'

'What's that mate?'

And as he put his head closer to Ben's face, Ben brought his fist up fast. He felt Todd's nose give a satisfying crunch. He had a few precious seconds to get away but when Ben tried to jump up, his legs just slid out from under him, buckling. Banti had done more damage than he expected. Ben collapsed. Any second now Todd would recover. This was going to hurt. He almost smiled – this was a first – he'd never been beaten up twice in one day.

But before Todd could react the telephone cabin door was pulled aside. 'What izz going on 'ere?'

Todd, his nose beginning to pump blood, turned savagely on the hotel owner. 'You stay out of it, froggy, if you know what's good for you!'

But if Bertrand was worried by Todd's threats, he didn't show it. He drew himself up to his full height, which wasn't much, admittedly. "Ow dare you frettin me in my own country! You do not scare me you miniature Breetish 'ooligan. And I am Belgium, not French!'

'Well, whatever you are, you'll be sorry in a minute.'

Todd's hand moved towards a small zip-up pocket in his jacket.

'Not so fast, I sink. Ze poliss, zey are on zere way and looks like you will be caught red-'anded at zis rate.' Todd paused. They were in an open square. Too many witnesses. Todd may have been furious but, unlike Ben's mother, he was always in control. He grabbed Ben's hair.

'You'll keep.' he hissed in his ear, before getting up and sauntering away, ignoring the blood that ran down his face. Bertrand calmly watched him go and then turned to Ben.

'Well mister staying-out-ol-night, climin' op-ze-drainpipes, getting-beated up, it seems I aff 'elped you again.'

'Didn't ask you to,' said Ben thickly, batting away Bertrand's pudgy hand, as he staggered to his feet.

'Ah know,' said Bertrand, more kindly, 'but 'ere I am anyway. But if it was not for zis young lady,' he gestured behind him to someone Ben hadn't noticed, 'this oll may aff been a lot worse!'

Millie took a big side-step around Betrand. 'I saw it across the square. I thought Banti was going to kill you, I'm amazed you can even stand! Here, let me help you …' but Ben shoved her away too. 'Fuck off!' he snapped. Millie jumped back, as if Ben was wired up to the mains electricity.

'But, your head is bleeding again, we've got to get you to the doctor … we've got to tell St John, or the police … you may well be tough but you could be seriously hurt – I've seen it on TV, people who get kicked die of haemorrhages.' But Ben was already ignoring her. He turned and put the now dead phone back on its hook and pushed past them both.

'I told you once already. Leave me alone. I don't need your help.' He stopped and studied their faces. 'And I really don't need your pity, either – it's … it's dirty.' Then he turned away.

• • • •

Ben started to run.

He ran until his chest heaved painfully, Banti's kicks already swelling his ribs, making his breathing agonising – sharp stabs of pain that felt as if his splintered ribs were gouging holes in his lungs. But he didn't stop until he had left the town and crossed the canal, eventually coming to a ragged stop outside a large building that looked like a warehouse.

Peeled and faded blue paint across the top of a building next door said, *Obourg Gare*. Somehow, for some reason, it felt like a destination. A strong instinct, one he had learned to listen to over the years, told him this is where he must be, that he had to get into the deserted warehouse.

He came to a side door half-hanging off his hinges. His chest heaving painfully, he pushed the door just wide enough and slipped inside.

• • • •

CHAPTER 19

Extract from the journal of Corporal Sam Lyle, 4th Middlesex Regiment. • • • • • •

24th August 1914, Mons, Belgium.

By 6am the attack had cranked up again. 8am: heavy German losses right across the canal front, with bodies strewn all over. Our rate of fire sounded almost as if machine gunners were straffing the German lines but it was nothing but single shot Lee Enfields fired by trained soldiers. Brave men.

Mid-morning: it almost looked like the Lieutenant was right - quick fire, doesn't matter if it is bows and arrows or 303 rounds - counts more than numbers. For one mad, euphoric moment it looked like we was winning!

And just when it looked like we'd pull it off, everything fell apart.

The Lieutenant noticed it first. "Why in God's name didn't our engineers blow that bridge?" I followed the line of his arm and saw right off what he was talking about.

Just about 100 yards off, a swing bridge hung open on its huge hinges. An invitation if ever there was one.

All the others had had their swing mechanisms smashed but they'd been in a hurry and missed this one.

"Jerry'll have to get that down if they're to cross the canal ... but if they get that bridge to lie flat they can use their heavy machine guns to set up covering fire and they'll be able to swarm over. Our lines'll be overrun in minutes."

Somebody on the other side must've had the same idea. No sooner had Lieutenant Goddard spoken then a German gunner opened up to the left flank, answered by one in the centre and some rapid German rifle fire from the extreme right. It was all concentrated on the hundred and fifty yard stretch we was on. For a full minute none of us could do anything but keep our bleedin' heads down and prey. There was a brief cessation in the fire and Charlie chanced a quick look over the top.

"Blimey sir, looks like you were right!"

At that I stuck my head through a gap in some sandbags and saw a large chap - one of the Bosch infantry who'd been firing at us all night - his grey-blue uniform standing out against the trees still in full leaf. He was going like a steam train down the hill. The first shot on our side was about three foot to his left and the second kicked up some dust no more'n a few inches from him. "Either that fella's got a death wish or 'ees the bravest blighter I've ever seen in combat," remarked Charlie, with a low whistle. "Bet you a sovereign to a shilling he'll never make it."

The lone German infantryman jinked a bit as another shot tipped his helmet off his head but carried on regardless. Down the hill, all the way to the embankment. I saw then that although he was going fast, he was fairly old for a line soldier. Thirties - about my age, I was guessing. A couple more shots came from someone in our lines and the German dropped his rifle. Against all odds he was nearly at the bridge now.

"Don't seem right, shooting an unarmed man," said Charlie and I agreed. Bullets still kicked up the earth all around him but we watched mesmerized, as he finally got to the bridge.

"Hero or not," said the Sarg, shouldering his rifle taking aim, "if he gets that bridge down, we're all dead men." He paused allowing his arm to steady and took a deep breath. As he breathed out, I saw his finger squeeze the trigger ever so gently and the rifle kicked. We all switched out attention to the German who had leapt onto the bridge and was tugging at a lever that would release the pontoon. The German seemed to jump slightly and slip.

"Got 'im!" exclaimed the Sarge with satisfaction, but, as he leant down to prop his Lee Enfield against the side of the dugout, Charlie cleared his throat.

"Must've just winged 'im Sarge – 'cos e'es only gawn and got up again." And sure enough, when we looked up he was back on his feet. From where we was I could see blood pumping out of his shoulder but he was a big lad and it didn't seem to bother him much. The Sarge swore under his breath and shouldered his rifle once more but just then the covering fire from the German lines found its range again and we all had to duck down. By now we was all beginning to panic – the German was an hero all right but he had to be stopped. The machine gun from across the canal ran past our dugout and this time Charlie was on his feet fastest.

It was a hard shot now, Jerry bullets peppered the air and he only had a second to sight and fire. But if anyone can take a shot under pressure its Charlie. He let off one round, ducked down, working his bolt action as he did so, popped up and fired again.

"Did you get 'im?" asked young Tom, eyes wide.

"Dunno, that last one felt about right..." just then we heard the sound of metal grating on metal and a bang.

"That's the bridge going down!" hollered someone further down our lines and sure enough there was a ragged cheer from the German side, who knew a victory when they saw it.

Their machine gunner had stopped firing for the moment, so we all risked looking over the top. The bridge was down and so was the brave German soldier.

His body had fallen in the water and he was floating face up, as pink bloom of blood and water spread slowly about him, like the petals of a poppy.

"Looks like you got 'im, after all," I says to Charlie, "but we was too late. That bridge is open and the Bosch'll be over it once they get their troops sorted."

"He'd get a Victoria Cross for that if he was British," remarked the Lieutenant drily. "Here," he scribbled off a note and handed it to Tommy, "take this to the command centre, they need to know... and wait for orders!"

The next twenty minutes was like purgatory.
A boy Tommy's age could be forgiven for leaving the dugout and running all the way 'til he got clear of this terrible place, back to the Channel and all the way home. And no-one would blame him. But just after midday, with the Germans now pouring fire on our positions as the massed troops ready for an assault on the bridge Tommy comes running back, gasping for air, sliding into the bunker as Jerry bullets flew zapped around his head like angry wasps.

He handed the Lieutenant a note and we all held our breath.

"OK, chaps, we've been ordered to fall back!" shouted Lieutenant Goddard over the din.

"Thank gawd for that," remarks Charlie, spitting sideways.

"I dunno, I was just getting comfy," says George.

"Yeah, sure you was – well if you 'ang about you can offer the Bosch your services when they get over the canal."

"Righty ho," says George cheerfuly, he paused, "what as?"

"Clown," says Charlie, shouldering his pack. Always last in, first out, our Charlie.

Truth was (although none of us would admit it) we was all in a terrible hurry to leave and our spirits picked up no end at the thought of putting the dugout and that hell that was the canal far behind us. Best news we'd had in two days. Even young Tommy perked up.

"Where to, Sarge?" he asks. The Sergeant exchanged a look with the Lieutenant, who was studying the map. Then he looks up, and smiles at the young lad.

"You've bought us some luck, young man," he says, tapping his pipe on a spot on the map where I can see a train track marked. "We're being sent to Obourg Gare, just about the only defensible position for miles by the looks of this thing." Tommy looked pleased as punch at the complement. Then there was this pop.

Looking back, "Thankyou Sir," was what I think he meant to say but something just sort of caught in his throat and his thin little shoulders sagged forward. The Lieutenant looked up and frowned, sort of puzzled.

"I say, young man, are you quite alright?"

"Fine sir," Tommy tried to straighten up but a great well of blood suddenly spilled out from his nose. Tommy looked down at his shoes where all his blood had fallen. He looked like he was going to cry. "I'm really sorry sir..." was all he managed to say before I caught him in me arms. Oh, no, no, no, I was thinking all the time as I laid him down ever so gentle. Not him, not Tommy, I looked at 'is poor little face it looked even younger, he's just a little lad, this ain't right, it can't be.

Funny some bullets you hear and some you don't. The ones you don't are usually the ones that do for you.

The Sarge took control first – the Lieutenant just stood there, looking shocked to his core. "Right everyone, fall back, NOW, before anyone else gets shot, and keep yer 'eds down!"

As we ran back though a park with benches that ran along the canal, I saw several plumes of smoke coming from the town that had been at our backs. The Bosch must've already got up there, all the way to the main square, around our left flank. The town was on fire, the battle was lost...

About a mile down the road we came to the station and an old warehouse next door, all boarded-up to stop looters. There were already about a hundred or so of our lads from the Middlesex taking up a defensive posts in the station: windows were being smashed out and sandbags hastily piled up around the frames to make firing posts. I saw a Maxim gun being positioned in a ground floor window, belts of gleaming ammo in rolls strewn around it. Defensively, it was better than the canal but I knew there and then we would probably die here – too many enemy and too few of us. The town was wrapped in an orange and black fog of fire, sparks and dense smoke. They would be coming down the hill for us soon...

Poor Tommy was still alive but coughing and sobbing as more blood oozed from his shoulder than I would have thought possible could come from such a skinny wreck of a body. I cast about but there were no signs of stretcher-bearers or medics. The Lieutenant took out his hanky and wiped the grime from Tommy's face. "Don't worry, old chap, we'll soon have the quack over to take a look at you. You'll be on your feet in no time. Hospital grub is pretty decent I'm told ... you'll get a chance to put some weight on."

In answer Tommy smiled, but when he tried to speak but just coughed some more dark blood.

"Poor bugger, 'ees a gonner, I reckon," said Charlie, well within earshot. The Lieutenant whipped around.

"Less of your loose talk Private, thank you very much, unless you want to end up on a charge..." Instead of apologizing, as he should have done there and then, Charlie looked like he was going to say something back. The tension built, and then Charlie gave Lieutenant Goddard a murderous look but at least had the sense to keep quiet or perhaps he was just about to say something when a small voice cut across the scene.

"Sir?" The Lieutenant kept his eye on Charlie for a moment longer as if daring him to answer back. Then he turned to Tommy, softening his expression.

"Yes, Tommy?" No rank, just his name.

"I think I am dying, Sir and I'm scared, Sir."

The Lieutenant shook his head emphatically. "No Tommy, you're not a doctor, none of us knows that for sure. Things are a bit muddled now but we'll get you some medical help — they can work wonders in the field these days." He turned to me and Charlie. "Corporal, take Tommy into the warehouse and get him comfortable, he'll need to rest and there's too much going on in the station." I nodded, shot Charlie a glance and we picked Tommy up as carefully as we could.

When I looked back, I saw this terrible look I'll never forget on the Lieutenant's face.

It took a few goes but we bust the door down and soon got Tommy rested on some old sacks in a first floor room overlooking the road into town.

By now his face had gone a sort of milky grey

colour. His teeth chattered but he seemed to be in less pain, half-conscious.

But just as Charlie moved over to the window to check the Bosch advance, Tommy's eyes opened wide as he stared at something behind me. He mouthed something but no sound came out and he gripped my arm tightly. I knew then that this was his final moments, I'm a professional soldier - you see - I'd seen it hundreds of times. And this time, with young Tommy, I knew I'd seen enough. My chest felt the crushing weight of pointlessness. I'd just reached the end of my tether. This was what despair felt like.

As Tommy closed his eyes he sort of sighed and his head slumped forward. I cradled him for a few moments longer, thinking of our own boys, I couldn't hardly help it, then I looked up and saw that the ghost - the boy with strange clothes - was back. He was staring hard at Tommy's face and I was shocked to see tears running down his face. Something about the way he held himself looked like he was injured himself.

I just stood there staring at him, Charlie didn't seem to be aware he was there or could even see him and I wasn't going to make a fool of myself by saying anything.

Eventually, with an effort, the boy tore his gaze away from Tommy and looked at me. Right at me!

I knew there and then that he wasn't really a ghost, they don't feel pain for the living. Then a thought just popped into me head — angels do...

. . . .

CHAPTER 20

•••• Room on the first floor

Ben had run, when he saw the young soldier dying and the look on the old soldier's face – of grief and despair … then recognition when he looked at Ben. They were both in this together. Ben now knew that to be the case, too. But had no idea why … or how.

So, that night Ben went back to the warehouse.

He was past caring now about being caught by anyone; the only thing on his mind was to find out why this was happening. He had never seen someone die before and it had shocked him to the core – not so much the blood but the uncertainty in the boy's eyes. That the corporal could see him made a difference. Ben now felt sure that he had something to do in that warehouse and however much he was scared of going back there, whatever horrors awaited him, he knew he had to go. He had some part to play, he was sure.

As Ben crept down the deserted street, it seemed to him that the warehouse didn't so much resemble a building but something almost alive, hunched in the darkness – a concrete and metal monster whose broken widows resembled empty eye sockets and whose gate gaped at him like the jagged maw of an injured animal.

Ben was so preoccupied with his thoughts that he didn't notice the shadow that followed him.

Then, he was back at the side door, which he forced open, wincing as the heavy metal made an unnaturally loud noise when it scraped against the stone floor. Slowly, with extreme hesitation, he trod the stair to the first floor as the dark figure behind him slipped silently through the gap he had left.

In the bowels of the stairwell, with no streetlight filtering in, it was pitch dark and Ben had to grope his way blindly to the first landing. He paused there for a moment, letting his eyes grow accustomed to the gloom. He thought he heard a brief scuffing noise but when he looked around sharply he could make nothing out, so he had no choice but to continue his journey upwards, onto the deserted first floor to where pale moonlight lit the room in strips.

No pile of sacks strewn across the floor, no soldiers, nothing … but yet something made the hair on the back of Ben's hands stand up. Something told him to be wary, to be afraid. He stiffened as he felt warm breath on his neck.

'Hello Ben.'

• • • •

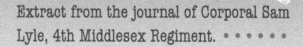

CHAPTER 21

Extract from the journal of Corporal Sam Lyle, 4th Middlesex Regiment. • • • • • •

24th August 1914, Mons, Belgium.

When I turned around, Charlie was looking at me. He had this queer expression on his face.

You know, I don't think he'd even noticed Tommy had just died, but then something told me he wouldn't have cared even if he had. Slowly, deliberately, he picked up his rifle, his eyes not leaving mine for a second. I was about to ask him what was up when he pointed his own weapon at his OWN foot and fired. The noise echoed in the confined space, deafening me, so missed hearing the ricochet. Wouldn't have made much difference though. As I said, you never hear the bullet what's got your name on it. It must have bounced off the floor, then off one of the girders above us. Next stop, Charlie's bullet it hit me in the side, just below the ribs. I smelled cordite and felt a sudden pain like I've never known before. Some say that at first they don't feel they've been hit, it's only when all the blood starts squirting about they realise they need medical attention.

Some old soldiers speak of it like a thump, followed by numbness. Lucky beggars, I say – this felt just like I'd just been shot by my best friend in the stomach.

I looked over at Charlie who was staring at me. His foot was a mess – he'd done it on purpose to get out of the war the easy way. The coward's way. I know he didn't mean for me to get hit too but it made no difference.

"Sam!" he says, gritting his teeth through his own pain, "I'm sorry," he paused and stumbled. "Aargh, me foot feels like fire! I never meant for it to get you too. Are you hit bad?"

I looked down at the blood pumping through my fingers, and was almost relieved to see more blood coming from the back of my tunic. It looked like the round had gone right through my body and out the other side – a clean wound at least. Must've clipped a rib on the way through, it hurt like a freezing dagger being shoved in my side each time I breathed.

"'Ere, let me help you..." Charlie pulled off his tunic and limped towards me.

"STOP!" I yelled at him "– you just stay away from me Charlie Peave!"

"Ah, Sam, nah don't be like that, it was an accident, looks like you'll survive too. I done you a favour, got you out of this mess early on. I tell you, this war's goin' to turn nasty, take my word for it ...

I feel it in me marrow."

I turned on him, my head suddenly clearing as I felt boiling anger rise up and push the pain in my side into the background. "You're a liar, Charlie! You swore the King's oath to fight and now you've gone back on that!"

"I can't do this anymore, Sam"

"Do what?"

"Fight a war for a bunch of toffs I never met, who wouldn't even stoop to shake me hand if we ever did meet, for a war I don't understand the reasons we're fighting. It's just politics and them royals having a family ding dong — 'cept plates don't get smashed if you're really important and you have a fight wif your cousins, it's ordinary people like us get smashed instead."

"What about Belgium?"

"What about Belgium, how do I even know all that stuff about burning civilians is true?" I looked about, my eyes being drawn to the boy who lay dead in the room. "Ok, then, what about young Tommy here he was real and he was barely sixteen, I'd say an 'e had more guts than the both of us. What you've just done is made his death a mockery, like it didn't mean anything!"

At that point I was angry with Charlie but probably angrier with myself cos, deep down, I saw this point. I'd done India, then Africa and now this. Three continents, three different wars and none of them seemed to change a thing. I even agreed with him about this one being not like the others. There was something about the ferocity of the German army facing us and I knew we'd only beat them by becoming as bad as them or worse.

But I still love my country and I'm proud to be born English.

"I'm not a coward and we're paid to do a job, Charlie, so we do it."

We stared at each other: Tommy was dead, we was trapped here in this warehouse and the Bosch would be on our doorstep soon and I was shot.

"Well, Sam." There was something about Charlie's voice that set a warning bell off in me head. I looked up. Charlie's eyes had slitted, like he does when sizing up an opponent, working out there weak spot. Any second ... there! He licked his top lip, under his thin moustache, that's Charlie making his mind up. Something had suddenly changed in the room, between us. Inwardly I shuddered. "Sam, me old pal," he repeated, softly but clear as a whistle. "If you're not with me on this ... you know what that means don't yer?"

I swallowed – a minute ago I had been angry, but now I was terrified of Charlie. I needed to get out, away from Charlie but, just then, a wave of sickness hit me and I staggered a bit. I leaned heavily against a concrete pillar. "Look Charlie, truth is we've been through it all together and I owe you my life. It's not what you're doing, you're just trying to survive, like we all are, but the way your doin' it — it's not right and I can't stand here and say anything different."

"In that case, you're more the enemy to me than the Hun." And he pulled his cutthroat razor and lashed out at me.

The blade on the shaving razor was keen enough to cut through steel I reckon. He was standing quite close but not close enough and his injured leg slowed him down. Charlie with a knife in his hand was a terrible enemy normally, quick as a whip. Luckily, I knew most of his moves — I'd seen him fight countless times — and I managed to swing out of his way as the blade missed my throat by a hair's breadth.

I wasn't so lucky with his next cut that caught my arm, just above the left wrist. It wasn't as bad as the pain in my side but the razor sliced through my thick tunic and cut into my flesh, almost to the bone, it felt, and I cried out.

"Charlie!"

"I can't take the risk Sam, on you blabbing, maybe not now but p'raps in a few years to your misses, or your mates when you've had a few pints. They'd shoot me like a stray dog, you know that ..." Charlie moved towards me like a hyena going in for the kill.

• • • •

CHAPTER 22

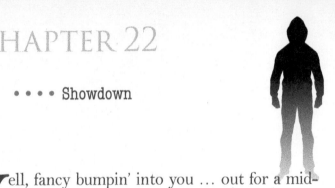

• • • • Showdown

'Well, fancy bumpin' into you ... out for a midnight wander were we?'

Slowly, Ben turned around, although every fibre in his body was telling him to run. Light from the moon poured through the window and he could clearly make out Todd's features. His white face and his grin, picked out in harsh shadows, looked liked a death's head.

'I thought someone was following me.' It was all Ben could think to say at that moment.

'Time to pick up where we left off Bartops.' Todd's arm shot out and Ben felt something very cold and very sharp rest against his exposed throat

Ben swallowed, willing himself to stay calm. 'That's unlike you Todd – I never had you down for a knife man.'

''Dis be di right tool for di righteous job ... an' you keep getting' away from me.'

'Been ... *aaaa' aah*,' the knife edge pressed harder against the soft, exposed flesh of his throat. Ben swallowed nervously and tried again. 'Been busy, Todd.'

'You can say that again.'

Ben felt the point of the knife prod deeper and a trickle of blood ran down to the collar of his t-shirt. He winced and licked his lips, which had just gone very dry. 'Well, it's a bit extreme but you've got my attention.'

'Got a job for you, blud.'

'You mean if I won't nick hand bags offa old ladies for you you're goin' to cut my throat? Come off it!' Ben swivelled his eyes at Todd; he was genuinely incredulous.

'Oh no, we're beyond that now, *way* beyond that. I spoke to my dad this afternoon. This is big boy stuff now. Need someone who's not a family member to pay him a visit now and then – you'd like that wouldn't you Ben, visit me dad, just like old times?'

Ben arched his neck as far back as it would go. 'Yeah, sure thing, Todd, I'll pop in and see him when I visit dad.' This seemed to please Todd, who relaxed his arm and Ben felt the blade pull away from his throat – no more than a millimetre – but Ben was grateful. A hair's thickness either way could mean the difference between life, or bleeding to death.

'Good lad! Now once in a while I might ask you to bring him a little parcel. Nothing much, you'll easily been able to fit it in a sock or hide it under your arm. They hardly don't search minors, see – especially not if they're just a family friend – an' he'll be so grateful – help him an' he could help your dad … an' your mum.

He's getting' to be quite important is Dad, especially now he's in for ten straight. Got to look after yourself in prison … you know that Ben.'

'You mean drugs, don't you?'

Point of the knife went deeper and more blood flowed.

'That's none of your business now is it? – an' don't fink you can run blabbin' to your dad. Turns out 'ees gone all goody two-shoes too, wants to turn over a new leaf for his family an' all that cobblers. You know what Bartops! Lately, your family really make me sick!'

Just then the door crashed open.

If Ben had been expecting St John, or, better still, Bertrand with a few policemen for good measure, he was about to be disappointed. Both the boy's eyes had got well used to the light by now and they could make out the unmistakable figure of Banti lumber into the room. He was carrying something that looked heavy in his right hand. Some sort of container. Ben had no idea how long he'd been there, listening in the stairwell. He assumed he'd followed Todd, the same way Todd had followed him. But this did *not* look good.

'Banti!' Todd smiled but he didn't look pleased either. Banti, always a bit unfit, was puffing. 'Awright? Saw you leavin' the 'otel, thought I'd shadow you … make sure you were alright an' all.'

'Oh yeah … we're just fine … just two old mates

catchin' up.' He turned back to Ben and winked. 'So you run along now Banti,' he carried on, his eyes never leaving Ben's for a second. Banti stopped abruptly.

'What?'

'You 'erd me Banti, mate, I'm busy.' In the half-light Ben saw Banti's shoulders droop. If he hadn't been covered with bruises because of him, he would have almost felt sorry for the larger boy.

'An' I 'erd you too, Todd,' replied Banti, sounding hurt but staying put for now. 'Let me do the running for your dad – drugs, guns, money … you name it.'

'Sorry mate, he don't know yer, won't trust you nevir.' Banti moved forward again and Ben's eyes went to the jerry can he could now see in his hands. Ben wondered what was in it. He also wondered why Todd didn't notice the danger signals from Banti – he guessed that his ex-friend must have been too intent on Ben to care.

'No, I can do it, anyfin' for your dad, 'e's a legend, 'e is.'

'Nah, you're aright, Banti,' Todd's voice was deadpan, noncommittal. 'No really, mate. I don't know why you're even asking this loser. I keeping tellin' ya – I'll do it.'

Todd now looked angry. 'I *said*, you're alright, Bar-tops 'ere is doing … '

But Banti was too upset or perhaps stupid to give Todd some space. 'I can do it, just give me a chance, anyway, you don't mean your dad don't trust me,'

Banti's voice rose in hurt, 'what you mean is *you* don't trust me. Never give me the time of day until that little squirt wouldn't do what you said anymore!'

'Carefully now, Croft.' Todd's voice carried real menace now but Banti seemed past caring.

'Or what? You seem a bit tied up right now with your friend. You can't tell me what to do neither ... couldn't stop me doing this, for example!' He tipped the jerry can and some liquid sloshed out.

'What are you doing now?' the menace in Todd's voice was suddenly tinged with the faintest hint of alarm. Ben didn't blame him, the contents of the can smelled strongly of petrol. When he answered, Banti's voice had suddenly changed to a mumble, as if he was speaking to himself.

'Sometimes someone in me own 'ed talks to me. It whispers, so I can't hear, but sometimes louder. When I get angry about something they tells me to burn fings ... you know. It always makes me feel better that does. That's how I got kicked out of my primary school ... I set light to the play shed. It was plastic and the smoke was all black and wavy, like the sea was made of tar and it was floating up into the sky. Beautiful. I feel awright when I can see fings burning. An' I brought this along to show you I had it in me.'

'Had what in you, Banti, what are you plannin' you fick lump?'

Banti carried on pouring the contents of the jerry can around the room as if Todd hadn't spoken. He doused the centre of the room and around the door. '… if I set light to this building, then you'll know I'm serious. An', an' …' he seemed to be thinking something through, 'we'll burn 'im,' he jabbed an angry finger at Ben, 'an' say he did it – he's mad, just like his mum!'

'Banti …' the point of Todd's knife moved away from Ben's throat by another precious fraction, 'can't you see I'm busy 'ere … don't be more of an idiot than you really are!' Banti stopped as if Todd had slapped him.

'Idiot?' he yelled, 'idiot, idiot, idiot, *idiot*, *IDIOT*, moron, scope, mong! Don't fink I 'aven't 'eard it all already. *Barmy Banti* – there's another for you …'

Ben suddenly realised why Banti had always gone on about his mother, why her mental illness seemed to make him so angry, so aggressive.

' … serve 'em right I tried to torch the place and all of them in it. I can see it in you're your eyes, I'm just some a fick nutter. That's what you fink isn't it? Well p'raps you can both burn.'

Ben and Todd stared in horror as Banti raised a huge meaty arm and flicked his thumb.

The lighter caught first time.

• • • •

CHAPTER 23

24th August 1914, Mons, Belgium.

With Charlie coming at me with a cutthroat razor and
my side bleeding and hurting so bad it was tempting
just to give up. I'd never beaten Charlie in a fight.
Ever since we was four, spending all day playing in the
gutter down our street, he'd been pushing me around.
Truth is, I only joined up, cos he told me too. And I
never admitted that to anyone before, not even meeself.

But something just went click in me head. Not this
time, I said to meself. No more! I wasn't going to give
into Charlie again. I owed you, and the boys and Poppit
more'n that.

I think Charlie was almost as surprised as me when
I hit him in the face. He staggered backwards a
couple of steps and yelped in pain as he placed his
injured foot badly. I moved forward but he was ready
this time and the cutthroat flicked up, just missing my
cheek and eye. I'd seen Charlie do that to a man
before, half blind him first and then cut his throat.

146

But Charlie was watching my hands and he didn't notice my feet. I trod on his bloody boot. "Aaargh!" he cried and then I kicked him as hard as I could in the knee.

The pain in my side was terrible but I was thinking clearly now and moving OK - the wound hadn't stiffened me up yet. All I felt was this anger against Charlie, not just for shooting me, but for everything, all the bullying, for all the times he scared me and for all the horrible things he'd done to other folk and I'd let him: because he was my friend, I always told myself - but really I was just terrified of him, same as everyone else.

As he went down, clutching his leg, I made a grab for the knife. My fingers were slick with me own blood but this huge anger gave me strength and I twisted it easily out of his hands.

He looked up at me, fear showing on his face now and for an instant I felt nothing but hate, I was going to slash those selfish features of his until nothing was left but a bloody mass. I raised my arm.

"Sam, no please!" It was shouted in a way so unlike him and it made me pause, just for long enough for my anger to ebb. He was at my feet, beaten. I could do what I liked, his life was in my hands to save or take. So I made a decision.

As I brought my raised arm down, I turned the

knife at the last moment and hit him across the jaw with my fist.

I dragged Charlie down the stairs, the adrenaline still pumping around my system giving me strength I wouldn't normally have. Outside I heard the company trying to get out, to retreat but when I looked up, I could see the Bosch coming down the hill fast. If we stayed put, we were going to be trapped, I could see that. I grabbed a passing stretcher-bearer. "Been injured, stray bullet." I says pointing at the slumped form of Charlie. "Then he fainted ... put him on your stretcher would you." The stretcher-bearer looked torn between helping and running but I must have looked serious cos he eventually nodded. For a moment I thought about following them. (I'd put on Charlie's tunic to hide my own blood.

"Are you hurt mate?" the stretcher guy looked at me. I did my best to smile. "Just nerves." He looked doubtful but nodded anyway.

Then I turned back and stumbled into the warehouse. I knew what I had to do to get out of the war ... but not like Charlie ... with honour.

And, in a way, I always knew this was coming. I had to die.

• • • •

CHAPTER 24

• • • • Trapped

If Banti had hoped for a dramatic gesture that would terrify Ben and Todd into submission, his elation was short-lived, and so was his position as the guy in charge. He must have been careless as some of the petrol had slopped onto his shirt and hands and they were still wet with fuel when he fired up his lighter.

He yelped, at first more in shock than in pain as a flame shot down his arm and set light to his clothes. Then, as the fire took hold of his clothes, he screamed and fell to the floor. Immediately he did so, the rest of the fuel he spread around the room caught and exploded in a rolling, tumbling mass of fire. Todd was enveloped, too, but Ben was shielded by Todd's body. Even so, the heat was briefly and seeringly intense, like someone had just held an electric fire against his cheek.

Todd cried out and fell to the floor, as the wall of flame quickly receded, the fuel rapidly burning away. Banti rolled and twisted on the ground still crying out but Todd was strangely quiet … still. When Ben looked down, he noticed the hilt of the knife sticking out of Todd's side. He must have stabbed himself accidentally when he fell.

Ben's first instinct was to make a run for the door, away from the fire, which terrified him. But the flames had caught some old sacking stacked by the exit and it was effectively blocked. He looked back at Banti who was still alight and, without really thinking it through, Ben ran towards him.

Reaching him, he grabbed Banti around the waist and did his best to smother the flames. Pain flared through Ben's hands and fingers and across his chest that was pressed tightly to Banti's smouldering shirt. Thick black smoke from the sacking was drifting across the room to where the boys were, making Ben cough and retch. With a huge effort he rolled Banti onto his back and then over again, putting out the flames that burned his clothes, which seemed to have stuck to his skin. He'd lost all feeling in his hands but he knew he must have burned them quite badly.

Ben glanced around and started dragging Banti towards the window. After about a minute he got him to the ledge and propped him against the wall. Banti was only half conscious by now, making small mewling sounds of pain. Ben then stood back and gave the window a sharp kick. It shattered, exploding shards of glass into the night. Gingerly, Ben pushed any remaining slivers away from the frame with his elbows and looked out.

Long grass. Thank God – and not too high.

By now the smoke was everywhere and Ben could only just make out Todd's body lying in the middle of the room. When he got to him Todd moaned and half opened an eye. He tried to push Ben away but Ben ignored him and grabbed the hilt of the knife with both hands.

Todd screamed as the knife came out – he knew you should normally leave these things in for the paramedics to remove but he couldn't risk leaving the knife in for what he planned to do.

Ben, still trying hard to fight the panic with the fire all around him, kept low, under the smoke. He dragged his friend alongside Banti, then he pushed the remaining bits of glass away from the sill and, taking Banti roughly under the arms, tipped him out of the window. He landed with a dull thud.

The fire must have caught some of the foam sheeting that lined the ceiling as it seemed to be taking over the whole of the room, scorching Ben's back as he tipped Todd out to safety.

His turn to jump now. Ben screwed up his eyes and forced himself to block out the memory of the fire at home and the coach. He straightened up to look out of the window, to work out where best to land but suddenly Ben felt faint, his legs buckling under him. He must have inhaled more smoke than he should and he realised he was about to pass out. Desperately, Ben tried to grab the window frame to steady himself but his fingers slipped and he fell backwards, hitting his head.

Just before he closed his eyes, the billowing black smoke pouring across the ceiling seemed to solidify into a human shape. Rough hands grabbed Ben's wrists and pulled.

• • • •

24th August 1914, Mons, Belgium.

When I got up to the first floor I had to rest. The bleeding in my side had slowed but I was feeling faint again and my cut arm, queerly, hurt more than the bullet wound. Even though this was all Charlie's fault, I didn't feel angry with him, I was glad, in fact. I had now repaid my debt to him. I was finally free of Charlie Peaves.

I staggered over to the window where Charlie had left his rifle and a box of shells. I checked my pouch and his - I had about sixty rounds in all. Not much but it would have to do.

Next, I looked out of the window and towards the town where I could see a line of German soldiers making their way towards the station in staggered file. It may have been an early autumn fog or perhaps smoke from the town but as they marched towards me, their legs and then torsos were slowly shrouded in mist, so it looked as if just line upon line of ghastly severed heads was tramping down the road like some terrible ghoul army.

This is it, Sam, I thought and I began firing into the fog. At first my arm was stiff and my firing was ragged but after a few rounds I loosened up. I could have still done with a Maxim and a roll of ammunition but my fire must have been on target because the advancing lines of soldiers halted and ducked for cover. I carried on firing, no longer seeing if I actually hit anyone but knowing that the longer I held them off, the more men from the Middlesex, who'd already been through hell over two days, could make their escape and re-group away from the town.

Then the bullets ran out. Too soon, I thought, too soon! I cursed myself for getting carried away, I could have fired a bit slower and kept a few rounds back.

For a few moments there was no sound, no return fire and I squinted into the mist. Slowly, the figures of the German infantry got back to their feet and began to march towards our position, some branching away to outflank our retreating men. I sagged partly with exhaustion but also in despair. I had failed. Some of our lads would have got away but not all. It was going to be the massacre Charlie predicted after all.

The mist began to clear and now more figures rose up. Rank upon rank in straight lines now. At their head a tall figure stood out proud and brave, a few feet in front of the other men but seemingly without fear.

But something wasn't right. I looked again.
They were heading towards the Germans in a jagged advancing line, Dorothy. I rubbed my eyes. At first I thought they had got confused up in the mist and general madness of the battle. But dark, brooding figures were now plainly visible. Most carried no weapons, 'cept for bows, most wore nothing more than old rags, tattered shrouds and torn capes - a ragged army carrying ancient weapons had sprung from no-where with a giant of a man leading them.

And the Germans fell back in terror.

Seeing their decrepit backs, I could only guess at the state of their ghastly faces.

But I didn't care, we had our reprieve. A ghost army with a huge figure at its head had risen up out of the fog and the Middlesex would have time to escape.

There was a bang, as if a shell had exploded in the upper warehouse. I staggered to one side as a ball of fire from nowhere ripped through the room. The planks were dry as old bones and a wall of flames sprang up in front of my face, obscuring the window, searing the skin on my cheeks and forehead.

I must have banged my head because I wasn't aware

of anything for a few moments and when I did open my eyes I'd lost all memory of where the door was and how to get out.

Through the smoke, I saw the body of Tommy, lying on the old sacks. Apart from his pale lips, he looked OK now, at rest. I crawled over and laid my hand on his young forehead. It was still warm and I felt like crying again, 'cept I didn't even feel I had the strength for that anymore. I knew I was dying and so I lay down on the sacking next to him. Smoke and fire now filled the room and I would soon suffocate. My last thought, as a dark, winged shadow, black as a crow's plumage, drifted across my eyes was whether I'd be seeing young Tommy meself in a few minutes.

I closed my eyes.

Someone shook me.

I felt more tired than ever in my life and in pain but whoever it was wasn't giving up that easily.

"Wake up!" It sounded like Tommy. I was dead, he was there to greet me.

I opened my eyes.

Through the smoke I saw the boy, the ghost or angel or whatever he was, his old burn scar plainly visible now around his eye and on his temple ... and this time I could hear him and feel him. It seemed as if the gap or door, or whatever allowed him to come and go had opened up wide and he was fully here. The fire! Somehow I knew that it wouldn't stay open for long. Behind the boy I could see the black shape gather itself into the form of a man, a huge chap in a poncho, with something sort of hunched behind his back. His eyes were visible for an instant through the smoke, pale blue, grim but not without sympathy. I recognised his lined face, I'd seen similar ones all my life in every battalion I had served in. He was a warrior. The Eternal Soldier. It was he who had led the counter attack through the fog.

Then the boy was dragging me out, half-lifting me, and pulling me along the dusty floor towards the door. My side screamed out in pain and I wished he would just leave me alone, let me be so I could slip from this world to whatever was next in peace.

"Don't die, don't die, please don't die," I heard him whispering under his breath, but I closed my eyes and let my body slump. "Come on!" he shouted now, "someone must care for you, someone will miss you if you just lie down here and burn to death!"

I that made me think of the boys, Poppit, you ... I thought of home. My leg kicked out as I tried to stand and slipped.

"That's it!" the boy gasped, he pulled me and I kicked out again, propelling myself towards the door. We staggered and toppled and I finally got to the stairs. No smoke now and I was able to look into his face. "Who are you?"

The boy looked taken aback a bit. By now we were at the foot of the stairs and then out the door. He laid me on the ground, all battered and bloody. The cool, fresh grass. I felt myself passing out.

"My name's Ben," was the last thing I heard.

. . . .

CHAPTER 26

•••• Mother

When Ben came around, it felt like he still had smoke clogging his lungs and he doubled-up coughing, feeling an odd-sharp pain in his side that came from nowhere he could immediately place.

Cool hands pressed him gently back onto crisp sheets and stroked his forehead. Gentle hands. Familiar fingers.

Ben opened his eyes and saw a face – not unlike his – looking concerned but calm. 'Mum.'

'Shh, the French doctor says you need to rest. No talking.'

Ben closed his eyes and was asleep in seconds.

When he opened them again, his mother was still there. It was morning but he doubted she'd had any sleep. When she saw he was awake, she reached out and held his hand. 'They rang me yesterday and said you'd had an accident. I came over immediately by train, the school paid. And I just sat here thinking about you, me, about Dad and how much has gone wrong and how much we have lost and I knew I couldn't lose you. So I sat in the carriage and all the time I concentrated on thinking, *be safe, please be safe, get well* – it's all a mother can do sometimes and those words went over and over in my head. And just as we were getting to the station I saw a huge ragged man staring at me and somehow I knew that he knew you and that he wouldn't be there, he'd be with you, if you were in any danger. I don't know why I knew that, it was the strangest thing and he just turned and walked away … and then I got to the hospital and it was night time but a lovely lady doctor said I could sit with you and although I could see you were hurt, she told me you would be fine.'

Ben nodded and squeezed her hand. He knew that she probably had no memory of their phone call but whatever sadness and rage she was feeling then had now passed. She was more like her old self than he'd seen in months.

Ben hurt pretty much all over but, for once, his heart had stopped aching.

• • • •

CHAPTER 27

• • • • End and beginning

One month later…

Ben wandered down the street, clutching a book. He was in a pretty good mood actually. Hallowe'en was in a few days and everywhere in the shops and petrol stations there were pumpkins, scary masks, ridiculous masks and fireworks for sale. For the first time in living memory, Ben wasn't dreading all the bonfires.

The only obvious outward sign of what had happened in the old warehouse was a slight limp in Ben's left leg. The worst injury by far had been his hands where he had beat the flames on Banti's body: all the lines on his fingers and hands had been scorched away. Todd had really liked that, when he'd found out – if you left no fingerprints, then you'd never be caught by Old Bill!

Todd had been in the same ward as they were convalescing. Things would never be quite the same again between them as when they were in primary together but he had a funny feeling he'd know Todd for the rest of his life. The scarring on Todd's face would never fade but it kind of suited his features and over a game of chess he'd admitted it was a good reminder of what had nearly happened but didn't thanks to Ben. 'I reckon that's enough to keep me on the straight an' narrow for now. Even me old man finks so.'

Ben's surgeon warned him that he may walk with a limp forever. Ben didn't mind, like Todd, he also felt he'd had a lucky escape, although one which he would never fully understand. The last thing he remembered was dragging the corporal to safety. He guessed that the archer, or angel – or whatever he was – had actually saved Ben when he got him out of the warehouse in his own time by pulling him back to the corporal in the First World War. It still all seemed so impossible that to re-live those few days was to wonder, all over again, about his sanity, but Ben's memory of that night was little more than a blur.

That the angel was a force for good was not even obvious. Ben's best guess was that he really was an archer, a sort of ghost or spirit left over from Agincourt. He assumed he only appeared to English people.

Ben knew he would never see him again but he wondered if he still appeared to others who needed him. And how many other guardian angels there were out there.

Legion.

• • • •

Whilst in hospital, even St John had visited - along with his orange wife who'd bought a large box of chocolates in a *Lidl* carrier bag. At first the school had been wary (*prob'ly fink we'll sue*, according to Todd) but when they realised Ben wasn't going to blame them for the fire or Banti going mad and trying to kill them, they'd become generous – even going so far as to offer him free extra tuition to catch up before going back after half term. There was almost no chance he'd be thrown out now.

After about a week of being there, he woke up very early one morning to see a bulky shape at the end of his bed. Ben's dropping eyelids snapped open – *the archer!* – but, as he blinked the night time gunk out of his eyes, the silhouette clarified into somebody less alarming and even more familiar.

'Dad!' Ben, suddenly felt almost completely better.

"ello Ben, my boy. 'ow are you 'oldin' up?'

'They've let you out early!' Ben was ecstatic. He wondered if mum knew. His dad gave a short, cynical laugh and glanced at the two men in uniform who were standing at the end of the children's ward.

'No such luck. They've let me come and see you – compassionate whatsit.' He had a twinkle in his eye that Ben remembered.

'What?'

'Got some good news, though son. Some of me mates from the football came to see me the other day. As soon as they heard I had been nicked again they picked up our boat and hid it in the clubhouse. It's all painted up, the anti-fouling done as well – tidy and ship-shape – for when I get out in six months.'

'Great!' said Ben and he really, *really* meant it.

After that they'd talked about Mons and his dad asked for more details about what happened but Ben glossed over the bits about the corporal and claimed a bang on the head and a dodgy memory when it came to Todd.

'Well 'is dad won't forget it – reckons you're a bleedin' 'ero, an' I do n' all. 'Ee's a bit rough round the edges, but 'e's a good mate to 'ave on the inside, thanks to you savin' 'is son.'

Ben said nothing.

After about half an hour Ben lay back on the sheets and watched his dad go back down the ward towards the prison wardens. 'Ta, ta Ben,' he said cheerfully turning by the fire doors at the end. 'See you in six months.'

His most frequent visitor though, apart from his Mum, had been Millie.

• • • •

Ben had spent the long hours in hospital reading up history books on the First World War, especially those talking about Mons and thinking about everything that had happened in Belgium. He thought he knew who the corporal was now and although he'd come no closer to unravelling the mystery of the Angel or Archer, he had a theory about what had happened he wanted to test, which explained the reason for his destination that day as he walked along the road looking at all the Hallowe'en stuff.

• • • •

Fludd St, E11, said the sign as he turned off a busy main road down a quite terraced street. He remembered the address from the front of the book he'd seen the corporal writing in. Number 6 was easy to find, it was the only one that remained unpainted, standing out like a blackened tooth in a row of healthy dentures. Old rubbish bins blocked the entrance to a front garden that was clogged with weeds and yellowing newspapers, and for a moment Ben thought the house must have been deserted.

He knocked without much hope of an answer but was surprised when the stained glass in doorway darkened and, after some faffing with several locks, an ancient face peered at him through gap in the open doorway limited by a brand new chain. For a moment he thought it was the corporal and he almost panicked but a halo of white hair, like threadbare cotton wool piled into a wispy bun, made Ben realise that he was looking at a very old lady

'Yes?' she said and then a hand shot to her wrinkled mouth, 'oh my lord!' she exclaimed.

• • • •

Half an hour later he was sitting in a surprisingly neat and clean front room, being served milky tea in a chipped china cup.

Ben took a sip of tea, just to be polite and then opened his bag. Inside was a book, *The Story of the Angel of Mons*. He cleared his throat. 'It says at the end, at Obourg station, that a soldier from the Middlesex regiment stayed behind to provide covering fire. He saved the rest of the men in his battalion but they never found out who he was.' Ben paused, the old lady looked somehow close to tears but was smiling at the same time. The last thing he wanted to do was upset her. Ben took a deep breath. 'That was your dad wasn't it?' The old lady nodded, unable to speak. 'It also says the unknown hero probably died but he didn't ... did he?'

'How do you know?'

'I don't. I'm just hoping – it's the only thing I've really thought about for weeks. I pulled him out of the smoke but the next thing I knew I was waking up in the hospital, now ... in my own time.' Ben paused. 'I still don't understand what happened.'

'Father had a theory,' the old lady took a small hanky from inside her sleeve and dabbed her eyes. 'He thought that sometimes, for the briefest of instants, time sort of stretches and gaps appear and sometimes people walk through them, into another time but just for a few moments, before they're pulled back to their own time. It's like ghosts.' Ben nodded, although he didn't really understand. For now he focused on just one thing, the thing he had been thinking about for weeks. 'So he survived?'

The old lady nodded, almost gleefully. 'Yes, he came back to us! To his family, it was all he ever cared about really. But even after what he had been through, he still wanted to go back to the Great War, to the trenches but he was badly burned, you see and the wound in his side never really healed. He couldn't fight anymore, so he stayed here and helped bring up his family. He was the best dad ever. But we never let on he was our real dad, there would have been too many questions about how he got out of France – his face was so scarred anyway, that most people wouldn't have known. Of course, folk in the area he'd grown up with, and the family, knew but no-one said anything, they knew he was a hero. People stuck together in them days.'

'And Charlie?'

'Never seen again, though Dad heard rumours he

went to Australia.'

Ben suddenly felt like laughing, a great weight lifting off his chest. Until now, he hadn't even known it was there. It all still didn't make much sense but for once life seemed to have a happy ending and that's all he cared about. The old lady leant over and touched Ben's hand. Her fingers felt very soft. 'My father described you to me so many times over the years, I knew it was you the minute I clapped me eyes on your face. Your burn ... you're not dead, are you?'

'No,' said Ben. 'I thought your dad was a ghost too, first time I saw him but if he could see me and told you about what happened a century ago, then I don't think he was.'

'He said you saved his life.' The old lady looked at him with bright eyes. 'and all I can offer you is a few Hobnobs to say thank you – '

'That's OK, it really is ... I just wanted to meet you, to make sure.'

The old lady looked confused. 'Make sure of what?'

'Um, I dunno, make sure it was all real, I guess. I know you're real and so was he and that your dad told you about me. I can't be going mad then can I?'

'No dear boy, I suppose not.' She paused.

'Have another Hobnob anyway.'

• • • •

After about half an hour, Ben made his excuses – he was expected home – he knew his mother would be waiting. It was his turn to pick up supper. Ben wasn't sure whether it would be a good day for her or a bad day but after everything that had happened – all that he had survived – he felt he could cope either way.

But just before he left, the old lady, Sam's daughter had a thought. 'I won't be a minute,' she said and left the room. A few moments later Ben heard her moving things upstairs.

When she came down again, she was carrying a battered notebook that Ben recognized instantly. 'I want you to have this,' she said. 'No, Dad would have been proud to give it to you,' she cut across the start of Ben's protestations, 'and you're in it – so that's proof enough, I'd say, that this all really happened.' She handed the notebook over.

Journal of Corporal Sam Lyle, Middlesex Regiment

was written in neat copperplate handwriting that Ben knew so well.

Ben thought it was probably the best present anyone had ever given him.

• *The End* •

For details on what really happened at the Battle of Mons in 1916 and the author's inspiration for writing the story, explore

www.monsterbooks.co.uk

or go straight to

https://www.monsterbooks.co.uk/middle-grade/the-angel-of-mons